#GOODGIRLBADBOY

BOOK 3 OF THE #BESTFRIENDSFOREVER
SERIES

YESENIA VARGAS

For my biggest supporter and best friend, Zendy. And for my daughters.

ONE

Nothing was better than the official start of summer. Unless you were destined to spend it without your friends.

Tori pulled into the drugstore on the way to my house. "This one, right?"

I nodded and leaned forward. "Yep, this is it. I love coming here. They have the best deals."

It had been just my mom and me for most of my life, so we'd learned to make money stretch. I couldn't exactly afford to walk into Sephora and buy the latest and greatest makeup, but I was pretty good at finding the best bargains at drugstores.

My friends and I got out of the car, the bright, hot sun beating down on us.

The school year had officially ended less than thirty minutes ago, and we were celebrating with makeovers and a sleepover at my house. But first: picking out makeup.

Across the parking lot, a lone guy skateboarded

this way and that, performing all kinds of tricks in the shade of a few poplar trees. I recognized him, in his familiar black t-shirt and blue jeans. His name was Emerson, and he shared my lunch period. Or used to.

Emerson jumped like he was diving into a pool for a swim, and I gasped. Then he landed on his skateboard upside down…and rode it like that, on his hands instead of his feet. He definitely seemed to be the most talented of the group.

"Wow," I said without thinking.

Everyone stopped, and Lena came up beside me. "What?" She turned her gaze toward the trees. "Isn't that Emerson Lopez?"

Tori shielded the sun with her hand over her eyes. "It's not a back handspring, but still…impressive. Didn't he get kicked out of school just last week?"

Ella shook her head. "Suspended."

Lena gawked. "Again? I'm surprised he hasn't been expelled yet."

Ella pursed her lips. "Just a matter of time."

Rey turned to me. "That boy has always been trouble. Ever since we were in elementary school."

My eyes widened in surprise. It was hard to imagine a second-grader getting into trouble.

Or how much abdominal strength Emerson had to have now to dive again, grab his skateboard from the ground, and do a backflip. Somehow, I found myself trying to picture how many rows of abs he might have.

Making sure I didn't have drool on the side of my mouth, I finally turned with the others to go into the store, but a middle-aged man with a round belly came out, almost running us over. We scurried out of his way.

He shook his fist in the air, taking several steps toward Emerson and his pals. "Didn't I tell you kids not to skate around here? There's a sign, for the hundredth time!"

It was true. He pointed to it, but Emerson and his two friends hardly glanced up at the guy.

The manager wasn't giving up, though. "If you don't leave, I'm calling the police. Don't think I don't know about the car you hit with your board the other day!"

Now Emerson stifled a grin, which only made the manager lose his cool completely.

"That's it!" the manager screamed, turning around and going back inside. The automatic doors hardly opened in time for him, and he almost fell.

I jumped forward to help, but he was gone.

Lena met my eyes. "Whoa," she said.

Ella blinked. "You talking about Emerson or the manager?"

Tori raised a brow. "Both. But that guy almost blew my eardrum out."

We turned back to Emerson, who made his way down the street on his skateboard, but he didn't settle for just cruising down the sidewalk.

Instead, he skated up to a small table outside a fast food place, rolled over the table on his back, board still in hand, and landed back on it. All in one swift move.

I had been sure he would crash and split his head open, but he was like some sort of Jackie Chan, using his environment to beat up his enemies, except Emerson was riding a skateboard.

His back was to me, so I didn't expect him to turn around and find me ogling him.

But he did.

Our eyes met for a split second, and I knew he knew I'd been staring. But he didn't laugh or smile. Instead, his gaze was intense like a hawk. His mouth serious.

My faced burned red hot, and it wasn't because I'd been standing outside for way too long. Nope, that was the sheen and sweat and color of pure humiliation.

Then he turned away, and someone else came up beside me.

Lena's loud voice rang in my ear. "OH MY GOSH, DID EMERSON LOPEZ SMOLDER AT YOU?"

———

I DRAGGED Lena away from the scene of the crime and into the store.

But that didn't stop Lena from going on about what had just happened. "You still have a crush on him, don't you?"

Ella came up to me. "Where have you been? Tori's been trying to explain warm vs cool skin tones to me, and I'm lost."

I opened my mouth to say something, but it was too late.

Lena was practically jumping up and down. "Emerson Lopez totally caught Harper staring at him. He gave her this super hot smolder. You guys *missed* it."

The mom at the checkout counter with her two young kids glared in our direction, and I pulled Lena toward the makeup aisle.

Then I tried to save face. "Okay, so I definitely wasn't staring—"

Lena nodded, completely sure of herself, and crossed her arms. "She was totally staring."

Tori held back a knowing smile, and I wanted to evaporate right then and there.

Ella tried to calm Lena down. "Lena, indoor voices, remember?"

We laughed, but my face still felt kind of hot.

Rey nudged me. "So you still got a crush on bad boy Emerson, huh?"

Everyone stopped goofing around and looked at me for an answer.

I stuttered. I stuttered bad. "Oh—uh, no," I scoffed. "No, no way—I'd never—"

Tori touched my shoulder. "You do. It's okay. We'll try not to judge." She winked at me.

Ella put her arm around me. "Promise."

Rey whispered in my ear, putting her hand up in front of her cheek so no one else would hear. "I don't blame you."

I didn't know if I should giggle or try to hide. No

way did I have a crush on Emerson Lopez. I had confessed thinking he was cute a few months ago at a sleepover, and I knew right away from my friends' reactions that he was bad news.

So no.

I no longer thought Emerson was cute. Not at all. Not when I saw him sitting atop his regular table in the cafeteria or when he roamed the hallways, chin up like he dared somebody to say something to him.

Nope.

"Normally, I'd be pretty excited at the thought of you going out with some really cute guy," Tori began, kneeling down to inspect some lip gloss, "but Emerson really doesn't seem like a good choice."

Ella smiled meekly. "I'm afraid I have to agree. He just doesn't seem like a very nice guy. And you're like the nicest girl I've ever met."

Rey nodded. "We'd hate to see him break your heart, Harper."

Lena sighed. "And then I'd have to break his face. So for my sake, Harp," she teased, "it's better to just stay away from that guy."

I wondered what could be so bad about Emerson, but at the same time, I knew they were right. They'd lived here their whole lives. There was a lot about him that I probably didn't know, even if part of me thought they had to be wrong.

Determined to find a good selection of products for my friends' makeovers, I looked for some discounted mascara, ready to be rid of the topic of Emerson.

But apparently, everyone else wasn't quite ready to move on.

Tori rubbed some lipstick on the back of her hand. "You know, all his older brothers were the same way. And I hear his younger brothers are already following in their footsteps."

Ella turned a tube of primer in her hand. "Yeah, it's a shame. They're all so handsome, but most of them have dropped out. I think their parents just don't care that they get in trouble all the time either." She turned to me and held up the primer. "What the heck is this?"

I pointed to the label. "Primer. It goes on before your foundation."

She blinked several times. "But it's called foundation. I mean, doesn't that mean it goes on first?"

"Think of this as your canvas," I said.

Ella's confused expression didn't change. "Huh?

Tori met my gaze and laughed. "We'll explain later. Just toss it in." She held out a green plastic basket.

I wanted to keep talking about makeup, but part of me was also curious. I'd never even talked to Emerson before. It sounded like there was a reason he didn't have the best grades or school attendance. Everyone seemed to focus on staying away from him. "So all his brothers have dropped out?"

Tori nodded. "Yeah, they were always getting into fights and stuff. I remember freshman year, his brother was a junior and the other one was a senior. They both got into a huge fight in the cafeteria one time, with three other seniors. And then Emerson jumped in too. Ended up with a black eye."

"Wow," I said.

"Plus he's a heartbreaker," Lena said, tossing a bright eyeshadow palette in our basket. "A total player. His older brother, the one who was a junior at the time, went out with my older sister. They lasted like two weeks and then he blew her off once he couldn't get what he wanted."

Rey shook her head. "Yeah, he doesn't sound nice."

I held up a container of foundation to the back of Ella's hand. "And Emerson is the same way then?"

Tori thought for a second. "He definitely gets into a lot of fights."

Ella gave me an unsure look. "And he's been known to go out with a girl for a few days and then break up with her."

Rey met my gaze. "He used to date Patricia, in my math class. She was crushed when he just broke up with her, like right away. He said he just didn't do relationships. He was her first kiss, can you believe it?"

Tori's voice went low. "And that fight he got into last week? I heard the principal tell Coach that if he doesn't get his act together, he's headed straight for juvie. He's on his last chance."

My stomach sank with the thought of falling for a guy and then being dumped. Maybe they were right.

I should definitely stay away from Emerson Lopez, as handsome as he was. The bad boy was off limits.

TWO

I brushed Ella's lashes with thick black mascara. "Are you sure you and your aunt can't take me with you to Puerto Rico?" Oh, the things I'd do to sunbathe on that island with tall, tan boys with foreign accents all around.

Ella gave me an understanding smile. "Sorry. Wish I could."

I glanced at Lena, who was expertly blending in eyeshadow for Rey. "Any chance you can stash me in the trunk of your car when you guys leave for Mexico?"

Lena giggled. "Sorry, With the size of my family, I'm lucky I'm going."

Tori swiped at something on her phone then put it down. "Unless you want to come with me to cheer camp this summer?"

"Yeah, right," I said. "Does it look like I'm even coordinated enough to do a basic cartwheel?"

Tori stared at me. "You can't do a cartwheel? I mean, can you even ride a bike, Harper?" she teased.

I handed Ella a mirror. "Finished." I grabbed my bag and pulled out some of my favorite makeup. "And to answer your question, Tori…sometimes."

Tori and Lena were very athletically inclined. Me? Not so much. But I liked to think I was a good friend, and that was more important, right?

I looked around at my four best friends in the world. "I can't believe I'm the only one not traveling for the summer. I'm so jealous," I said, imagining all the adventures they were sure to have.

Rey offered a smile from my bed, her usual journal right beside her. "At least you get two weeks with your dad, right? You get to ride an airplane back to Wisconsin."

I nodded. "You're right. I'm sure that'll be fun. The plane ride, at least."

Tori did Ella's hair in long, loose waves while I did my own makeover. When she was done, Ella stood up and twirled. "I love it."

As if on cue, the oven timer began beeping, and I sped off to the kitchen. The cupcakes we baked were cool enough to decorate. "Guys, come grab a cupcake!" I called.

Within minutes, we sat at the table, covering each of our giant cupcakes in frosting and sprinkles. I pulled out a single candle for Ella's cupcake, pushing it carefully into the center.

Ella beamed. "You guys are the best."

I dug around for a lighter while everyone pulled out their presents for her.

I sat back down, my own present in hand. I set it on the table and lit the candle. "We can't let you go off to Puerto Rico without throwing you an early birthday party."

The bright candle lit up Ella's face. "Do I get to make a wish?"

Tori smiled. "Of course."

Lena took tons of pictures, and then we all got together for a selfie.

We had to take it about twenty times before we were all satisfied, and by then, the candle had almost completely melted. But then we sang happy birthday, Ella made her wish just in time, and we ate our cupcakes.

"You guys are the best," Ella exclaimed. "This is so good."

"Agreed," Rey said beside me. "I can't believe you're already eighteen. I won't be eighteen until next spring."

Ella shrugged. "It feels just like seventeen."

I took a drink of water to wash down the frosting. "So is Jesse going to miss you tons or what?"

Ella nodded. "I'm gonna miss him too. But it's only a few weeks. Jesse has basketball camp. We're spending the day together tomorrow so I'm looking forward to that."

I turned to Tori. "What about you? Are you going to be pining over Noah for the next month?"

Tori sighed. "Totally. He's…the best." For

someone who had held in everything she felt for so long, Tori sure gave off all the puppy love vibes lately, but I was also super happy for her.

Those two definitely belonged together.

"I'm gonna miss all of you guys so much," Rey said.

Lena nudged her. "Just promise me you'll get one guy's number when you're on your trip."

Rey scoffed and opened up her notebook. "No way. My dad would kill me. And what's the point if I live here?"

Lena smiled. "The point is to have a little fun. You never know. I, for one, hope to break a heart or two this summer. That's why it's called a summer fling. It doesn't have to be serious."

Maybe for Lena it didn't. But I definitely wasn't Lena. I was hoping for the kind of guy who wanted more than to have a little fun. I wasn't sure my heart could handle the risk otherwise.

Ella's gaze on me caught my attention. "You sure seem pensive today."

I tried to shrug it off. "I just love seeing you guys so happy."

But that wasn't good enough for Tori and Lena.

"You need a little love in your life, Harp," Lena said, leaning forward and resting her arms on the table. "We need to find you somebody."

Tori peeled the liner off her cupcake. "I agree. Maybe the possibility of a cute boy is just what you need to make your summer a little more interesting."

I looked around the table, ready to invent some

excuse, but I couldn't come up with anything. Even Ella and Rey seemed to like the idea. "I don't really like anyone at school," I said, even if it wasn't completely true.

Lena didn't miss a beat. "You still don't know nearly everybody at school. Like the guys on the soccer team. Some of the varsity boys are pretty cute. I should totally set you up on a blind date."

And just like that, everybody chattered about how fun it would be to go on a blind date.

I tried to intervene. "I don't know, you guys. Going out with a stranger?" I had a feeling it didn't quite work like in the movies.

Rey looked up from her latest journal entry. "How bad could it be?"

———

IT TURNED out that a blind date set up by Lena could go very, very wrong.

But who could say no to Lena? Definitely not me. Saying no was hard enough most of the time for a people pleaser like me.

Lena had found someone in record time and called my blind date her going-away present. I just wondered who the heck had agreed to give up their first Saturday night of the summer for a blind date when most of the school was getting ready to jet off for the beach.

The rest of the girls wished me luck after getting me to promise to text them details ASAP. Saying goodbye to them this morning hadn't been easy, but at least I'd managed not to cry.

I distracted myself by trying on my new makeup and getting ready for tonight. Then taking my time getting to the meeting spot Lena had sent me. When seven o'clock finally rolled around, I was already waiting outside the specified restaurant downtown.

Then it was 7:15, and I wondered if I had gotten the time wrong. I checked my messages again. No, Lena had said 7 p.m., in front of Luigi's. This wasn't the fanciest place in town, but it was a step above fast food, and they served pretty good pizza.

By 7:30, I texted Lena that this guy was a no-show. I stood up to head home when a tall lanky guy walked up to me.

Putting my phone away, I stood up from the small bench I'd been sitting on the past forty minutes.

"Hannah?" he said.

Huh? "Um, I'm Harper," I replied, wondering if this was indeed my blind date for the night.

"Oh, right," he said with a laugh. "I knew it started with an H."

I cringed and gave him the best smile I could.

He had dirty blonde hair and wore a wrinkly button-up with some jeans. He seemed nice enough, but I had to admit I wasn't very impressed so far.

Maybe I was wrong, though. I reminded myself that he deserved the benefit of the doubt.

"Sorry, I'm late," he said, shoving his hands in his pockets. "I, uh, lost track of the time."

Both of my hands clutched my purse in front of me. "That's okay."

"Anyway, I'm Patrick," he said.

"Nice to meet you," I said, holding out my hand. "I'm Harper."

After a stiff handshake, we walked toward the restaurant.

Dinner was okay, even if it was a little awkward, but I looked forward to the movie, where we could just sit and spend some time engrossed in the latest blockbuster.

It wasn't *To All The Boys* or *Sierra Burgess*, but it was interesting enough.

At least until Patrick tried to hold my hand. The first time, I automatically pulled it away and brushed some hair behind my ear, hoping he'd get the hint.

But then, a few minutes later, he took my hand in his again, and I wondered how I was going to get it back. Within minutes, our hands were super sweaty, and I didn't know if it was him or me.

I wondered how much longer the movie could go on. Then I had the idea of excusing myself to go to the bathroom.

Scooting past him, I exhaled in relief and wiped my hand on my dress as soon as I was out of sight.

Once in the lobby, my phone vibrated with a new message.

It was from the #BestFriendsForever thread.

Lena: Hey, hot stuff. How's the date going? ;)

A winky face?

Harper: Um, not great TBH…

Lena: ???

Rey: What she said.

Ella: Is he a dud?

Tori: Oh no.

How to explain, I wondered.

Harper: Well, he was 30 min late. He got my name wrong. He did pay for my food and movie ticket, but I just wasn't feeling it, you know? I thought he got that, but then he held my hand in the movie just now. And I'm in the bathroom wondering if I can just leave.

Tori: OMG.

Ella sent an emoji with a blank facial expression, and Rey sent an emoji of Forrest Gump running away.

Lena: …

Lena: Wow.

Lena: Um, well the bright side is that it'll be over before you know it! Gotta run :)

Ella: Lol. Hang in there. Maybe it'll get better.

Rey: *shrugs* good luck

Tori: Can't get worse, can it?

THREE

It did get worse.

A few minutes later, Patrick found me near the concessions, and I mumbled something about being in the mood for some candy.

He took a step closer, his gaze going between me and the long line, where I clearly wasn't standing. I shoved my phone in my back pocket.

Pursing his lips, he said, "I think I know what's going on here."

My stomach sank. "You do?"

He nodded all-knowingly, slowly blinking. Then he met my eyes and said in a low voice. "You want to get out of here?"

I almost choked on my own spit. "Wh—what?"

"Like to the bowling alley next door? I don't know about you, but this movie sucks."

I almost laughed in total relief and somehow said yes before thinking things through.

Patrick led me to the bowling alley, and I

wondered how much longer this not-so-great date would last. My body ached for flannel pajamas, and my heart pleaded for Peter Kavinsky, even if he was just on TV and not here IRL.

But I sucked it up and tried to be nice. If you asked Lena or Tori, they'd say nice was my middle name, but I also didn't want Patrick to feel bad about cutting the date short.

After tonight, I'd go home, and Lena could let him down gently for me. I hoped.

Unfortunately for me, Patrick wasn't very good at bowling so our date didn't get much better. The thing was, I wasn't sure if Patrick knew he was bad. He just kept saying he was having an off night, but one could only accidentally throw the ball into the wrong lane so many times.

"Oops," Patrick said, abashed. "I'll go grab that."

But the ball was gone.

I picked up another one. "That's okay. Here."

He must have not been paying attention because, the next thing I knew, the ball slipped from our hands, and my foot erupted in colossal pain.

Trying not to yelp out in pain, I hobbled over to a chair and sat down.

Patrick followed me, and I made sure there was not another bowling ball in the vicinity.

He pulled up another chair and sat down. "Hannah, I am so sorry."

My foot throbbed too much for me to care that he'd gotten my name wrong again—yet he'd thought it was okay to grab my hand earlier.

I took in deep breaths. It had been an accident. No big deal. It's not like my toe was broken or anything. I hoped.

I gingerly slipped off the bowling shoe and my sock. "It's okay," I assured him, unable to meet his eyes.

Slowly moving my big toe, I exhaled. I was fine. The pain was already mostly gone. Even if my dignity was no longer intact. Talk about embarrassing. I'd gone on a few bad dates before, all back in Wisconsin, but this night was shaping up to be the worst of them all.

Patrick poked my big toe, and I winced in pain. I looked up at him in disbelief.

"All better?" he asked.

Why was he touching my toe?

I quickly put my sock back on, not bothering with the shoe. "I'll be okay." I made sure to throw in a smile. He genuinely seemed to feel bad about the whole thing. Besides, leaving in a huff wasn't exactly my style.

Patrick stood up with me, and we almost bumped into each other. "Let me make it up to you," he tried.

Now my smile was forced, and I wondered what else he had in store for me. "That's okay," I said. "It's no big deal. I should really get home anyway. I can't miss my curfew."

I glanced away, hoping my face didn't give the fib away. My mom didn't get off until midnight, not that I even had a curfew.

Patrick checked his phone. "But it's only nine o'clock." He sounded just as confused as he looked.

I made a point of hobbling off, but he followed me. "Uh, yeah, my mom is kind of strict about it. If I'm not home and in bed by ten, she'll ground me for like a month." I made sure not to make eye contact with Patrick, handing my bowling shoe over to the attendant on the other side of the counter. I took off the other shoe.

"Oh," Patrick said. "That's too bad. I've had a great time with you tonight."

I finally met his gaze. "Me too! But I should really get going."

I got my shoes back and put them on in record time.

When we got outside, I turned to face Patrick. His eyes slid down to my lips, which meant he probably didn't notice my bulging eyes. Then he started to come in, his glistening pink tongue clearly visible from this angle.

I leaned away. "Whoa!"

He stopped, confused again.

I pulled out my phone. "Look at the time. 9:40. If I'm not home in twenty minutes… I should go."

Patrick started to protest, and I stuck out my hand. He offered his too, and I shook it for half a second before saying goodnight and making my way to the bus stop like there was a buy one get one free deal on lip gloss.

When I rounded the corner, I grabbed my phone out of my pocket.

Harper: Lena, who the heck was that guy? He definitely doesn't look like he plays any sport. And he tried to kiss me! After dropping a bowling ball on my foot! So just in case you're wondering how tonight went, NOT GOOD.

Tori: OMGGGG hahaha.

Ella: Wow. Times a million. Is your toe okay??

Rey: The short story writes itself.

Lena: Um. Promise you won't be mad at me?

Harper: ???

Lena: Um, he's the...younger brother...of one of the soccer players. Sorry! No one was available. And I thought you could really use a night out with a nice guy. I didn't realize it would bomb so spectacularly.

Harper: Younger brother??? What grade is he in?

Lena: Um, ninth grade?...

Tori: I'm sorry but HAHAHAHA.

Harper: You set me up with a freshman????

Lena: HE SEEMED NICE, OKAY.

———

I TRIED to put last night's horror of a date behind me, but it was tough when my mom asked how it went the next day.

"So your blind date was a bust, huh?" she asked, slipping on some dangly silver earrings to match her knee-length black dress and heels.

I could see her reflection from where I lay on her bed. "Yep. Definitely a gigantic fail."

My mom turned around and gave me an

emphatic smile. "Sounds like Lena's not matchmaker of the year."

I laughed. "Definitely not. That girl should stick to soccer." And breaking boys' hearts, I wanted to say. Like me, she didn't have a boyfriend. Hadn't had one in a while, but that didn't stop her from kissing boys from time to time.

For funsies, she called it.

I definitely didn't kiss boys for funsies. If I kissed a guy, I really wanted it to be special and with the right person. Lately, I wondered if that special guy even lived in the same state. Maybe he was back in Wisconsin.

Or Australia. Or Japan.

Asian guys were pretty cute. But so was an Australian accent. Any accent, really.

The sound of the doorbell brought me out of my stupor.

My mom grabbed her purse and phone. "I'll probably be back late, so don't wait up if you don't want to. I'll call you, okay?"

I nodded, getting up and following her to the living room. I found a good spot on the couch as she rummaged in her bag.

"Keys, keys, keys…ah. Got them," she said.

She looked nice. It'd been a while since her last date, but she looked excited. "So what's his name?"

"Jake," she said with a smile.

"Cute?" I asked.

Her eyes lit up. "Very." She gave a quick spin. "How do I look?"

I stood up and gave her a hug. "Like a million bucks. Have fun."

The doorbell rang again, but she stopped before opening it.

"Oh, by the way, Ms. Moreau called yesterday. I completely forgot to tell you," she said.

My mom forgetting to mention that wasn't a surprise, but I wondered why Ms. Moreau had called in the first place.

"Your old transcripts finally came in. And it turns out some of your academic credits didn't transfer, sweetie."

My mouth fell open. "What? I'm still graduating on time, right?"

She opened the door, and a middle-aged man with a slight belly stood at the door with some flowers.

I waited for an answer to my question.

She smiled at the man and turned to me one last time. "Of course, you will, hon. But you will need to make up the three missing credits during summer school. You start on Monday. It's only six weeks. It'll be over before you know it. Oh, and don't forget to lock up behind me."

"What?" I yelled. I ran toward the door, but she was already gone. The door closed behind her.

My mom had a knack for forgetting stuff and not being very good at telling me bad news, but summer school?

I'd spend my whole summer making up credits I had already done back in Wisconsin?

I let myself fall on the couch, completely crushed inside. As if my summer wasn't bad enough.

All my friends were traveling, meeting people—probably meeting boys—and I was stuck here. But to top it all off, I couldn't even sleep in every day and watch mindless TV to make things a little better.

No. I had to go back to school on Monday. How much worse could this summer get?

FOUR

L ena's tan face stared back at me on my phone. "Summer school? Are you serious?"

It was the first #BestFriendsForever video chat since my friends had gone off on their travels, and already I had bummed everyone else out. Or maybe it was just me.

"Yep," I confirmed. "I have to be at school by eight o'clock tomorrow."

"That's even earlier than the regular school year," Tori noted.

I nodded. "By fifteen minutes. I have three credits to make up. An elective, like P.E. or something, a math credit, and a social studies credit."

Ella offered a smile, but it came out more like a grimace. "At least you get out early?"

An hour earlier than usual. It was something.

Rey's face appeared on my screen next. "And it's only six weeks, so it'll be over before you know it."

That's what my mom had said.

Lena piped up. "Yeah, and summer will be pretty much over by then too. That stinks."

Tori gave her signature eye roll. "Thanks, Captain Half-Empty," she said with a smile. "Hey, maybe you'll meet a cute new guy or something."

I thought about that, not fully convinced.

"At summer school?" Lena replied. "Only the students who fail too many classes to make up during the year go to summer school."

I groaned.

Now Rey grimaced. "Yeah, maybe not the best place to meet someone new."

"I just wish one of you guys was here with me," I said.

Life hadn't been easy when I'd first moved to Westwood High. It had been really hard to make new friends. Even back in Wisconsin, I hadn't had many friends, especially not a best friend. More like someone I talked to the most.

Her name was Kaylie, and she had someone else she considered her best friend. Which had hurt because, up until her confession, I had thought of her as my best friend.

But meeting Ella, Rey, Tori, and Lena had been the best thing that happened to me since I found out we'd be moving. I was going to be miserable without them for two months.

"You'll be fine," Ella said. "I bet those classes will be super easy for you, and if for some reason they're not, we're a text away. You know I love math."

Lena pretended to barf, and Rey snorted as she laughed.

"Thanks, guys," I said. "Keep your phones on you, because I'm sure I'll be telling you all how bored I am in class every day. And wishing I was at the pool or shopping instead."

Rey blinked back at me. "Just don't make new best friends," she teased. "What if we get back and you pretend you don't know us anymore?"

"Never," I replied with a smile.

"Don't let anyone be a bad influence on you," Tori said. "Like Isabella. She's been making friends with this girl at cheer camp who is not nice."

"Yeah," Ella said. "We love nice Harper."

Lena laughed. "Although I would be curious to see mean Harper."

"Yeah," I said. "Right. You guys know I'm like incapable of being mean."

Tori laughed. "That would actually be really weird."

"Yeah," Lena said, already laughing at her own joke. "It'd be like having a nice Tori."

BEING in school definitely wasn't the way I wanted to spend my summer. But after screaming and maybe a little crying into my pillow at six-thirty this morning, I knew I had no choice.

So I stepped off the bright yellow school bus and walked into Westwood High on what was supposed to be the first Monday of summer vacation. Only three other kids followed me off the bus. One guy had spent the entire ride snoring loudly and had to be prodded awake by the bus driver.

There were only three classes and no textbooks were being assigned so, according to the email I'd gotten, we wouldn't have lockers.

I grabbed my schedule in the cafeteria and made my way to the first class of the day. Math.

Or as it was called here, Applied Remedial Math.

What did that even mean?

I had no idea, but by the looks of the syllabus in my email last night, there was going to be everything from geometry to algebra to pre-calc and statistics. And lots of projects.

Unlike Ella, I wasn't a math whiz, but I'd gotten a B+ in math back at my old school. So I wasn't too worried, other than all the work I was going to be doing for the next several weeks.

I found my first class a few minutes early, so I looked around to see if I recognized anyone. There were only three other students, all girls, in the class at the moment, and they were huddled together talking in one corner. The rest of the desks sat empty, and the teacher, Mr. Nguyen, reclined back in his black faux leather chair with his eyes closed. He looked like he'd rather be home sleeping in too.

The sound of footsteps made me turn around. It was Ms. Moreau. She made her way to Mr. Nguyen, who sat straight up. He took the sheet from the counselor's hand.

"The final roster," Ms. Moreau said.

On her way out, she caught my eye and came right over. I gave her a small wave and smile.

"Harper!" she greeted me. "So good to see you. I'm glad you made it."

"Yeah. My mom explained the situation with some of my credits not transferring."

Ms. Moreau nodded sympathetically. "I wish there was more I could do, but this happens sometimes with out-of-state transfers. I'm afraid this is the only way for you to graduate on time. But from the looks of your grades this past semester, I'm not worried about you at all, Harper. You seem to apply yourself. However, if you run into any trouble at all, you let me know. I'll be here all summer."

"Thanks," I nodded. "So no summer getaway, then?"

She shook her head. "Not this year. But summer school is actually a lot of fun. You'll see."

She gave me a wink and was off.

A few more students strolled in and found seats in the back of the class. I sat in the third row, but I may as well have been in the front row. Everyone was in the back. And it obviously wasn't going to be a big class to begin with.

Just when I wondered if I should go back a row or two and attempt to find a friendly face, Mr. Nguyen stood up and started the class. I turned my attention to the syllabus in front of me so I could follow along.

Halfway through the teacher explaining the

project due in a couple of weeks, the sound of someone opening the door made us all turn.

I blinked several times, not believing who had just come in.

None other than Emerson Lopez.

He carried a skateboard in his hand and nothing else.

Several of the girls in the back started whispering, but it didn't seem to faze him. He found a seat three desks over and one desk back from me, setting his skateboard under his seat.

I turned back to the teacher, wondering if he was going to keep going.

Mr. Nguyen put his hands on his hips. "Glad to see you could make it, Mr. Lopez."

I glanced back at Emerson, who coolly gave a nod, hardly looking up.

Mr. Nguyen walked down the aisle and lay a copy of the syllabus in front of Emerson. Then he kept teaching.

I tried to listen, but my eyes kept wandering back to Emerson. Like most of the class, his gaze was anywhere but on the syllabus. Instead, his focus was on the window closest to him. Glancing out the window myself, I could see the blue sky, dotted with clouds, and the front of the school.

I wondered what Emerson was thinking about. It certainly wasn't math.

My eyes slid down his strong arms and the way his thin white t-shirt hugged his torso. From here, I could see the vein that traveled down his bicep. His mouth was set in a line, turned slightly down. His eyes were dark, but it wasn't just because they were brown, almost black. Whatever lay behind them was dark. Emerson's wavy black hair fell across his eyes, like a natural barrier to what he was thinking.

I sighed, just wondering and taking him all in.

As if feeling my eyes on him, he turned in my direction, and I quickly cleared my throat and pretended to read the syllabus.

He hadn't noticed me ogling him *again*, had he?

I really, really hoped not, because it had been bad enough that he'd caught me doing that the other day.

I took a deep breath and blew it out slowly, silently.

Staying away from Emerson was going to be a lot harder now that we had summer school together. What if he was in the rest of my classes?

No, it had be just math.

FIVE

Of course, it wasn't just math. He was in my social studies class too. But at least I made it through my second period without ogling Emerson too much.

At lunchtime, the cafeteria served as another stark reminder of how alone I felt without my best friends.

There were only about fifty kids in summer school, and several of them had taken off to find something better than the mystery meat and chocolate milk handed out by the lunch ladies.

The good thing was that we had a forty-five-minute lunch, way longer than the usual twenty minutes we got during the school year. The bad thing was that I hardly knew anybody in the cafeteria.

I scanned the mostly empty tables, hoping to find somebody—anybody—to sit with on the first day of summer school. It felt like my first day at Westwood High all over again. Even though the lunchroom had been packed then, it had been impossible to find a single friendly face in the sea of high school students.

Even after offering a wide smile to a group of girls, I had been rejected. "Sorry, this seat's already saved for someone else," had been the excuse.

Apparently, girls did that all across the United States, because I had definitely heard it back in Wisconsin.

I spotted a group of three girls I recognized from my math and social studies classes. Taking a deep breath, I made my way over, tray in hand.

The table was certainly big enough. I just hoped they'd let me sit with them.

Was there anything more humiliating than sitting by yourself in high school?

Probably not.

"Hey," I said with a smile, praying my voice didn't betray how nervous I was. "Can I sit with you guys?"

One of the girls, who donned short jet black hair, shrugged, but another one with long curly brown hair smiled back and said, "Sure."

I circled around and found an empty seat. "Thanks."

The hardest part of summer school was now over. "I'm Harper, by the way," I said, giving them a small wave. "I think we have the same classes."

Curly brown hair nodded. "That's right. I think you were in my science class last semester too. You're really smart, actually. Why are you stuck here with us?"

The rest of the girls waited for an answer, and I

tried not to stutter. "Oh, um, I just moved here a few months ago, and it turns out that some of my credits didn't transfer, so…"

Curly brown hair frowned. "Oh, that stinks. It's bad enough flunking a class. But passing and having to do it again anyway?"

Her friend, the one who had shrugged earlier, nodded. "Yeah, I would tell the principal exactly what he could do with my missing credits."

Curly brown hair turned back to me. "I'm Anna." She pointed to her friend. "This is Rachel. And that's Becca."

"Nice to meet you," I said, finally relaxing a little.

Anna sat up. "We were just talking about how hard it's going to be to pass math and social studies with Emerson in there. I could not stop staring at him the entire time." Everyone murmured in agreement, and Anna turned to me for a response. Her full lips curled into a smile as she waited for my reaction.

"Yeah, yeah, he is…very cute," I said.

"Cute?" Rachel said. "My little brother is cute. Emerson is…stupid hot. Like too much."

I nodded. "Yeah, he really is," I said, mostly to myself.

He was nowhere to be found now, which didn't surprise me at all. As soon as the bell had rung, signaling the end of social studies, he'd grabbed his skateboard and been the first one out the door.

"Did you guys see he didn't even bring a pencil?" Becca said. "Mr. Nguyen looked like he was going to blow an artery or something."

I laughed along with them, even if I couldn't fathom the possibility of not showing up for school fully prepared. I got anxiety if I didn't have extra school supplies in my backpack.

Anna took a swig of her milk. "I give him a week before he quits altogether. Last year, he only showed up for the first two weeks. He's really behind. I heard Ms. Moreau say that if he doesn't finish summer school and pass, he won't graduate."

"That's too bad," I said, the brooding image of Emerson from this morning coming to the forefront of my mind. Then I thought about what Tori said, about juvie being next for him if he didn't get his act together.

Rachel shrugged. "Not a surprise when it comes to the Lopez brothers. I don't think one of them has graduated high school."

Anna picked up her slice of pizza. "He'll probably be in juvie by the end of summer. His whole family is trouble."

So the thing about juvie wasn't a secret.

Then I asked, "Why do you say that?"

"I live down the street from them. Their dad is always in and out of jail. If you ask me, those three are going down the same path. I'm surprised Emerson hasn't been sent to juvie already. He never shows up to school. And when he does, he's getting into trouble."

Becca spoke up. "It's too bad. Such a waste."

Anna agreed. "Yeah. I've gone out with my share

of bad boys, but even I won't go near Emerson Lopez."

Rachel turned to me. "He hardly talks to anyone, much less girls. He's a loner. Better to stay away from him."

"Yeah," I said. "I've only lived here a few months, but it definitely seems like he's the one person to stay away from. But that's okay. I mean, he's not even my type, you know?" I tried to laugh, but it sounded kind of weird, like a scoff more than a laugh.

"You're definitely not his type," Anna said. "Believe me. He's not into good girls."

Rachel nodded. "I could feel your good girl vibes from like a mile away."

Becca took one of my fries. "You've got nothing to worry about."

The bell rang, and we got up. I followed after Anna and the others, their words still reeling through my mind.

They were right, of course. Just like Ella, Tori, and the others said. It was best to stay away from Emerson, no matter how cute I thought he was. Or how I simply couldn't tear my eyes away from him or stop thinking about his perfect hair, deep eyes, or abdominal muscles.

I blinked several times.

No.

There were three good reasons it would never work. I just had to remind myself of them every time I imagined what it would be like to kiss him, run my fingers through his perfect hair.

1. He was a rule-breaker, and I was a rule-follower.

2. He didn't do relationships.

3. Bad boys were the reason it was just me and my mom.

My mom had fallen for my bad boy dad back when they were teenagers. She'd never been able to get past him, not until well after I was born. And he had never stepped up, not as a partner or as a father.

All he'd done was break both of our hearts.

I took a deep breath. No way could I ever be interested in Emerson. I wouldn't make the same mistake as my mom.

No matter what it took, I'd make sure to stay far, far away from Emerson.

———

AFTER LUNCH, I checked my schedule on our way out of the cafeteria.

"General Elective?" I asked Anna in the hallway. "What does that mean?"

She glanced at my schedule then showed me hers. "No idea. Mine says Physical Education. So I'm headed to the gym."

Rachel stepped toward her. "Me too."

Becca held up her schedule. "I lucked out. I won't be running like you two. I got Childhood Education, which means I basically have inside recess the whole afternoon."

Anna placed her hand on her hip. "At least in

P.E. we can walk. Chasing little kids around all day who pick their noses and can't remember to go potty?"

"No, thanks," Rachel answered for her.

Anna winked. "Plus P.E. is like an easy A."

Becca smiled. "So is Childhood Ed. See ya."

I waved and turned to Anna and Rachel. "I'll see you guys later. I need to figure out where I'm supposed to go."

Anna gave me a wave. "Hopefully you get P.E. with us. There are tons of cute boys in there. We watch them play football."

And with that, she, Rachel, and Becca were off. It had been nice of them to let me sit with them at lunch today, but I was back to being on my own. It might not be the worst thing. They definitely weren't like my friends. Anna, Rachel, and Becca were rougher around the edges. Maybe I could bring a book tomorrow and read outside during lunch.

I found my way to Ms. Moreau's office and knocked.

She opened the door, a bright smile on her face. "Harper! What a nice surprise," she said, showing me in.

I took a seat in front of her desk, and she settled into her chair.

"What can I do for you, sweetie? Everything going okay so far?"

"It is," I said. "But I was wondering if there was some kind of mistake with my schedule." I leaned forward and let her take it. "It says third period general elective, but it doesn't have a room number or anything."

"Oh my, you're right. This is a mistake," she said. "Somehow, I missed signing you up for an elective. Let me take care of this now, and you can be on your way."

She tapped away at her keyboard for a few minutes. "Hm. Let me see what's still available."

I stifled a yawn and hoped I'd get something like Home Economics where I could bake cookies all day and learn the difference between a salad fork and a steak fork. That had been my favorite class back in Wisconsin. Definitely not P.E. I did not do well with P.E. And it didn't help that I had a knack for falling, especially when everyone was looking.

Like during the mile. I had almost finished in last place and then tripped at the finish line in front of the whole class. Just another good reason I had moved several states away.

Ms. Moreau cleared her throat. "Okay, it looks Physical Education is out of room. And so is Child-care 101. Down at the daycare, right next door. It's a shame. I'm sure you'd be great with kids."

I bit my lip. "Yeah, that's too bad. That sounds like fun."

Ms. Moreau clicked something else. "Okay, it looks like the only elective we still have available is a volunteer-based class. Kind of like Childhood Educa-tion. Except it's at the nursing home across the street. How does that sound?"

My mind immediately pictured a sunny nursing

home full of kind and charming senior citizens. "That sounds great," I exclaimed. "I love old people."

Ms. Moreau clapped. "Perfect!" Her printer spit out a new schedule. "Here you go. You're a few minutes late, but I'm sure you'll be fine. The manager, Mrs. Porter, is very nice. She'll fill you in on everything you need to know."

SIX

Apparently, not everyone loved old people as much as I did, because there was only one other student taking this elective.

And of course, it was Emerson Lopez.

When I walked in and saw him sitting in Mrs. Porter's office, I almost choked on my water.

The nurse who'd greeted me at the door led me there, and I took a seat next to Emerson, decidedly keeping my gaze anywhere but on him.

A woman who looked about my mom's age, but with a dressy blouse on instead of scrubs, sat behind the desk. She looked at Emerson first. "So, you're Emerson," she said, shuffling some papers.

He exhaled. "Yep."

Mrs. Porter turned to me next. "Which means you must be Harper. Ms. Moreau just called to tell me you'd be joining us. We're very excited to have you both."

I smiled. "Thank you. I'm excited as well."

Emerson caught my eye, and I chanced a glance at him.

He wasn't smiling at all. In fact, he looked annoyed to be sitting there, like he'd much rather be anywhere else.

Meanwhile, I tried to comprehend what the universe was doing. Every time I tried to stay away from Emerson, he ended up in my life even more.

I didn't get it.

But it was okay. We were here to help out at the nursing home. I needed an elective credit, as did he. It would be all business. I was sure he wouldn't even want to talk to me, if his current facial expression was any indication.

Mrs. Porter went on to explain the daily schedule at the nursing home, the different couple of wings, which one we'd be in, and some general guidelines we had to follow. Signing in and signing out. Making sure the front door always stayed closed because someone could get out and wander around. If they had Alzheimer's or something and didn't realize where they were, there was a good chance they'd try to leave.

So many things I had never even considered.

My grandparents had died when I was a baby, so I'd never even thought about all this stuff, but I couldn't even imagine what some of these elderly people went through. It broke my heart.

Mrs. Porter stood up, and I did the same. Emerson reluctantly so. "Okay, so you two will be in the elder day care wing. Right now, we're doing arts and crafts. In twenty minutes, we'll put on a movie for them. And then they get free time to play board games, knit, or anything like that until they're picked up."

She led us to the arts and crafts room of the elder day care wing. A single middle-aged woman with short hair walked around repeatedly explaining today's craft. It reminded me of a kindergarten classroom. Except these weren't confused and raucous five-year-olds. They were confused and quiet eighty-year-olds.

"I'll be around if you two need me. Don't be afraid to ask questions," Mrs. Porter said before taking off.

Without waiting to see what Emerson would do, I found an empty seat at a table nearby and sat down. Four blank and wrinkled faces stared back at me. "Hi, everyone," I said with a kind smile. "I'm Harper. I'm a volunteer from the high school. Can I join you?"

An old lady with wrinkles covering every inch of her face and wisps of snow-white hair leaned forward. "What was that? You're gonna have to speak up! My hearing's not what it used to be."

"Oh, um," I began. "I'm Harper," I said, my hand on my chest.

But still she didn't seem to hear me.

"What!" she shouted.

"Harper!" I said.

"WHAT?!" she said, loud enough for the entire room to hear, if they had been a decade or so younger.

Someone took the seat beside me, and I turned to

see another lady, much younger looking, beside me. "Don't mind her," she said. "She won't hear you no matter how loud you yell. Harper," she added with a wink. "I'm Ellie, by the way."

"Nice to meet you, Ms. Ellie," I sighed in relief at finding someone who could hear me.

"Relax, sweetheart," she said. "This isn't high school. Everyone around here is pretty nice. Except for me," she said, cackling.

I laughed nervously along.

"But I like you. You seem like a good girl."

Funny how often I'd been hearing that lately.

I observed Ms. Ellie. She was definitely the liveliest of the group, talking and laughing out loud several times throughout the craft.

I made my way around the table, helping several residents with the cutting and gluing of their felt picture frame.

While I did, I observed Emerson sitting awkwardly across the room, his back to me. One of the ladies beside him talked on and on, not caring that he never said a single word back.

The lady on his other side poked him with her glue stick until he sat up and helped her glue her decorations on. I stifled a laugh and went back to my own table.

Ellie talked my ear off until it was time for the movie. "Oh, I hate this one," she said. But she found a seat near the front anyway.

Ms. Nancy, the nurse, came up to me. "We usually do their snacks at this time."

I followed behind her. "I'd be happy to help."

We served cheese crackers for those who still had their teeth—or dentures—and Jell-O for those who didn't.

Ms. Nancy handed the plastic cups to Emerson. "Mind passing these out?"

He took them without a word and left.

"Not really a talker, that one," she said quietly.

I shook my head and stared after Emerson. "I don't think so."

After thirty minutes of the movie, half the nursing home was snoring, but we gently woke them up for free time.

Ms. Nancy checked the clock on the wall. "Do you two mind assisting me? I need to get everyone into the main room."

"I'd love to," I said.

She smiled at me. "Oh, having you two around is going to be a huge help."

My heart grew about two sizes.

We made sure everyone made it back to the main room and got them situated.

Ms. Ellie grabbed a game of checkers and sat down to play with a man who looked a few years older than her. I waved goodbye to her, then headed to the front to sign out.

Emerson was already there. "Glad that's over," he said.

I did a double-take, not believing he was talking to me. "Oh, um, I thought it was fun. Beats doing math equations."

He shrugged. "Beats cleaning up litter alongside the road, I guess." He grabbed his skateboard from a corner of the office, ready to leave.

"Oh, um, I didn't realize that was an elective, not that I would have picked that either," I said, trying to recover.

He turned back to me. "It wasn't. Ms. Moreau said I could do my community service here instead of on the freeway if I showed up to summer school."

I nodded, thinking volunteering here beat community service. And juvenile detention too.

"So you failed math and social studies too?" he said, still facing me.

Surprised he was still talking to me, I replied, "Um, no, actually. I just moved here last semester, and three credits didn't transfer. I kind of need them to graduate on time."

He seemed impressed by that, the fact that I wasn't here because I had flunked. "Wow, so you actually want to be here."

I nodded slowly. "Um, kinda. I'd like to graduate," I said with a laugh.

"Oh," he said. "I was hoping maybe you'd cover for me if I bailed tomorrow."

I blinked several times, my mouth open.

He went on. "I mean, you can skip, too, if you want. If you were planning on bailing too. But they might figure out what we're up to if neither of us show up."

I finally found my voice. "Uh, no, thanks. I really need these credits." As much as I'd rather spend my days at home trying on makeup and watching rom-coms.

Emerson shrugged. "I need these credits, too, but I also don't want to spend my afternoons building puzzles and serving Jell-O."

I grabbed my backpack and followed him out the front door.

By the time I went down the steps, he was already several yards away. The sound of his skateboard on the gray concrete reached my ears.

According to my new schedule, I was going to be spending most of my day with the school bad boy.

This was really shaping up to be an interesting summer. Deep down, I knew I should be careful around Emerson, but a bigger part of me lit up at the thought of spending time with him.

SEVEN

"You're doing homework?" I heard from behind me.

I turned to find Emerson looking over my shoulder with a smirk. My heart immediately sped up at the fact that he was standing so close to me, just inches away.

He nodded at the math worksheet in front of me.

"Um, yeah," I said, tucking my hair behind my ear and trying to focus once again on the math equation in front of me. It was movie time at the nursing home, and we had a good twenty minutes of free time. Of course, I was going to take advantage of the time to finish my homework.

He sat down beside me, but instead of sitting down normally, he spun the chair around first and rested his arms on the back of the chair. "Do you always do your homework before you even get home?"

I stared back at him, a little confused. "Do you prefer to do it at home?"

He smiled, and I tried not to gasp upon watching his pearly whites revealed to me. "I prefer not to do it at all," he whispered. Then he leaned back and crossed his arms.

Finally understanding what he really meant, I said, "If you did, though, you might not be in summer school in the first place." I couldn't meet his gaze when I said that.

"Ouch," he said. "So you are capable of saying something a little mean."

I looked back up at him, and guilt flooded my stomach at the thought of him thinking I was being mean on purpose.

"Fine," he said, pulling a wrinkled sheet out of his backpack. It turned out to be the math homework due tomorrow. "I'll let you be a good influence on me."

He glanced at my paper, and I covered it up. He burst out laughing. "I wasn't trying to copy off of you. Geez. I just wanted to know your name."

"Oh," I mumbled. I moved my hand.

"Just kidding," he said with a grin. "I already know your name. Harper. You seem to have this math thing down."

I turned my paper over this time. "Well, good luck copying off me now. But I'd happily help you figure it out, if you let me."

His eyes twinkled like he was in on some joke. "You'll happily help me, huh?" he said. "Okay, Harper. How about you help me?"

He slid his chair closer to me, and my heart rattled around in my chest like a wild horse.

Slowly, I turned my paper over again so I could look at the problems.

Emerson swept his hand through his hair, and my breath quickened. Why couldn't I make sense of this math problem all of a sudden? The numbers may well have been hieroglyphics.

"I kind of meant today," he said.

"Right," said, exhaling. "Um, let's start with this problem. I think the first thing you need to do is simplify."

By the end of the movie, our math homework was done, and I somehow hadn't made a complete fool of myself in front of Emerson.

"Thanks," he said, shoving his homework back in his backpack. Then he stood up to help those in wheelchairs back to the common room.

A few minutes later, while I built a puzzle with Ms. Ellie, he played a game of chess with an older gentleman.

"Looks like we both have good taste," Ms. Ellie said, giving me a wink.

I blinked back hard at her, then I realized what she meant. Shaking my head furiously, I said, "Oh. No. I don't—"

"Honey, you don't have to hide anything from me. There's no shame in finding someone attractive. You're young. Now's the time to take risks when it comes to love. Oh, if I were only seventeen again…" Her eyes glittered, and her lips curled up into a smile.

Ms. Ellie got this far-off look on her face like she was remembering something fun—and maybe a little reckless.

I held back a grin and went back to the puzzle of the Eiffel Tower while she daydreamed of her past. Dozens of little pieces littered our small table, but I managed to find the one I needed. My triumphant glee brought Ms. Ellie back down to earth.

"What was I saying?" she asked me. "Ah yes, being young and in love. Harper, you've got to live while you can. Before you know it, you'll be old like me. Now, I've still got it," she said, primping her dyed blonde hair, "but not everyone is this lucky. Don't be afraid to tell a boy you like him."

My face felt hot, and I only hoped her loud voice hadn't carried all the way across the room to Emerson. I didn't need him thinking I liked him.

Because I definitely didn't like him.

Ms. Ellie went on, talking about the right way to ask a boy out, and I tried to follow along.

Meanwhile, I looked in Emerson's direction. His attention was still on the chess game with Mr. Roberts, the senior citizen he seemed to like best. The only senior citizen here he seemed to like. Maybe because, like Emerson, he was pretty quiet, although his eyes were kind and bright.

Emerson's brows knit together in concentration as he stared down at the board and all its pieces. He moved a tall piece and said something to Mr. Roberts, who laughed. I couldn't help but smile at their interaction.

If I got to know Emerson and maybe become friends with him, that was different, way different than liking him. After all, we'd be spending a good part of our summer here at the nursing home. How could we not end up becoming friends?

There wasn't anything wrong with that, right? Just during summer school.

———

"I'M NOT sure how I'd feel about working with old people," Lena said, pursing her lips and aiming her eyes at the ceiling. "Don't they fall asleep all the time?"

I laughed, and the rest of the girls smiled. It had been over a week since they'd left me to fend for myself, but they were making good on their promise to stay in touch. "Sometimes, but they're so sweet. I'm really loving it. I'd been hoping to volunteer some-where this summer anyway, so I guess it worked out for the best."

Ella crossed her legs in front of her laptop. "I wish I could get school credit for playing with puzzles and listening to old people tell stories."

Rey gasped. "Me too! Oh, I'd love the chance to write stuff like that down. Can you imagine every-thing they've seen throughout their lives?"

Her far-off look reminded me of Ms. Ellie. "Oh, you'd love it there, Rey. You should totally come with me when you get back. I definitely plan on volunteering on the weekends once school starts. You too, Ella."

Tori cleared her throat. "So who else is in this elective with you?"

"Um, not a lot of people…Just one, actually. You'll never believe it," I said, wondering why talking about this made me a little nervous. "Everyone else went for P.E. or volunteering at the daycare down the street. But only me and Emerson ended up at the nursing home. No one else wanted to hang out there, I guess."

I played with a cookie crumb on my bed, evidence of my afternoon snack.

Lena's voice reached me loud and clear, even though she was a whole country away. "Wait, what?"

Ella and Tori looked like their eyeballs might pop out of their sockets, and Rey's mouth hung wide open.

Lena's shocked face filled my phone screen. "Did you say Emerson? And you're just now telling us?"

I shrugged. "It's really not a big deal. We don't even really talk," I said. Other than doing our math homework together most days. That didn't really count, did it?

No one said anything for a moment, and I wondered if they believed me. "Anyway, he seems kind of nice. At least with the people at the nursing home. He definitely doesn't get into fist fights there, if that's what you're wondering."

The look on Lena's face said that wasn't quite what she was wondering, though.

Ella pressed her lips together. "Yeah, everyone has a nice side."

Rey nodded. "Uh huh, no one's all bad."

But they didn't sound completely convinced.

"Don't worry," I said, offering them a small smile. "We're not friends or anything. Like I said, I barely talk to the guy. It's just another class."

Even though it was really three classes.

Tori nodded several times, appearing completely serious. "Uh huh."

Then Ella jumped in with a question for Rey about where her family was headed next, and I almost sighed out loud in relief at the change in topic.

I hadn't expected my friends to react like that just for mentioning Emerson's name. Like they said, nobody was all bad, and maybe they had only ever seen this one side of Emerson.

The way he helped Mr. Roberts from place to place around the nursing home and made sure nothing on the floor could make him fall. That said so much more about him.

Or how he opened the little Jell-O containers for everyone without being asked.

Everyone saw the side of him that was silent and brooding, but Emerson was an iceberg. You'd be completely wrong if you thought that what was on the surface encompassed who he was.

I was sure that if my friends could see this side of him, they would see that there was a lot more to Emerson Lopez than they thought.

EIGHT

I signed in at the nursing home and knelt to pull a pencil and notebook out of my backpack.

Emerson came in, his skateboard in hand. He nodded at me, and I smiled as I stood up.

He glanced down at my notebook. "What's that for?" Then he grabbed the pen on top of the clipboard, scribbling his name under mine. When he was done, he turned back to me.

"The social studies project? I decided it would be a good idea to interview someone here, maybe create a poster," I replied.

We started toward the arts and crafts room, his eyes on mine and his mouth turning up at the corner. "The social studies project? You mean the one the teacher just told us about today?"

I could tell he was holding back a snort, and I pursed my lips. "It's due in a couple weeks, and I'd like to get started sooner rather than later."

Now he chuckled. "Let me guess? You're gonna turn in your poster at least a week early?"

Stuttering, I managed to say, "S—so?"

He laughed full on then, and the sound made butterflies erupt inside my stomach. I was making Emerson laugh, and all I wanted was to make it go on forever.

But then he was off to his usual table with Mr. Roberts. Just like that, he was gone, and I found myself aching for his presence again.

Shaking that thought out of my head, I found Ms. Ellie at a nearby table, already recounting stories from when she was young.

I smiled, glad I'd remembered to bring my notebook. Thanks to her, I'd have plenty of primary source material for my social studies project.

I explained the project to her, and she practically jumped up in her seat, clapping from excitement. "Oh, I have so much to tell you, Harper." She winked at me and picked out a peach-colored pencil for today's project, sketching out a fruit bowl in the middle of the table.

Once she got started talking, I couldn't get Ms. Ellie to stop. By the time the craft of the day was done, I had a few pages of notes down, and she said she had more for me when it came time to do our puzzle.

During their movie time, I sat at a table in the back and looked over my notes, drawing little stars over quotes I wanted to write out in big letters on my poster.

Emerson sat down beside me. "No math homework today?"

I shook my head. "Didn't you hear Mr. Nguyen today? We just have to study for that quiz tomorrow."

"There's a quiz tomorrow? Hmm, I was wondering if tomorrow would be a good day to skip class or not, and I think I just made up my mind," he whispered.

"Yeah, it definitely wouldn't be a good idea to skip. Quizzes makeup 15 percent of our grade," I reminded him, getting back to my notes. "I'm going to go over my math notes as soon as I'm done with this. I can quiz you if you want."

Emerson leaned in just a tad. "I think you misunderstood. I'm thinking *because* there's a quiz tomorrow, I probably won't go to class."

I looked up at him, and he was right there. "Wait. You're skipping *because* there's a quiz? That doesn't make sense."

The sound of soft snores and the movie reached my ears as I waited for Emerson's response.

He shrugged. "What's the point of showing up if I'm just gonna flunk it? May as well hang out somewhere not surrounded by four blank cement walls."

Huh? I closed my notebook. "Why do you think you'll flunk it? You've been doing great on the homework."

Emerson leaned back in his seat, his gaze on the movie. "Quizzes and tests aren't really my thing."

Not sure what to say to that, I exhaled. Finally, I

said, "I bet you could pass that quiz if you really tried. You're smarter than you think."

Then I opened my notebook again, but it was impossible for me to concentrate. I turned back to Emerson, who was still watching the movie. "So are you just not going to do the social studies project either? I mean, no offense, but…" I searched for the way to say what I was thinking, but they all sounded wrong.

He looked at me. "What?"

Now it was my turn to shrug. "It's just—I know you can do this." You just don't want to. But no way would I say that part out loud.

Maybe it was enough to make Emerson mad, but I was glad I had said something, even if he hardly looked at me the rest of the afternoon.

———

EMERSON DIDN'T SHOW up for class the next day or the day after that. He didn't show up to the nursing home either.

Becca was sure he was gone for good. "Just like last year," she said. "Watch, I bet he won't graduate with us. He wouldn't be the first. His brothers didn't graduate either."

I didn't like that she always had something negative to say about someone, and I was glad when Becca and her friends went off to their electives that afternoon.

Arts and crafts time was almost over when the

front door opened, and in came Emerson. His eyes met mine for a second before he made his way to the front desk to sign in.

He was back to his brooding quiet self, because he didn't say a word to me.

At least, not until the last few minutes of the movie.

Abandoning his chair in the corner of the room, he came over and sat at my table. "Hey," he said.

I glanced at him and tried to figure out the next step on the math problem in front of me. "Hey."

Even though there was a movie playing, the silence between us felt huge.

I shifted in my seat, trying to think of something to say. "Haven't seen you in a few days."

He nodded.

Again, more silence.

I tucked my hair behind my ear. "What made you decide to come back?"

He glanced away, and I wondered if I had said the wrong thing.

Just as I opened my mouth to change the subject, he said, "I really need to graduate."

I nodded.

"Which means I need to pass these summer classes."

Offering a small smile, I said, "I can help you if you want."

His eyes met mine, full of surprise. "You'd do that?"

Wait, what was I signing up for? Hadn't I told my

friends—and myself—that I'd stay away from the school's resident bad boy? And now I was volunteering to be his tutor?

But the hopeful expression on his face—and the leap my heart did because of it—meant it was impossible for me to say no. "Of course. We're in the same classes anyway. Doing the homework, studying for the quizzes, and getting those projects done really won't take as long as you think." I thought of that last day of school at the drugstore when he'd glided on his skateboard down the sidewalk like it was a part of him. "I promise you'll still have plenty of time to skate around or whatever."

Emerson's smile was back, and this time, it reached his eyes. "Skate around?"

I felt my face turn pink. "Isn't that what it's called?"

He laughed, the low sound penetrating through my chest. "How about you help me study for that math quiz I missed?"

"I thought Mr. Nguyen didn't do make-up quizzes and tests?" I said, pulling out my math notebook.

He sighed. "I have Ms. Moreau to thank for that. I think she baked him cookies."

"Sneaky," I said, opening my notebook to the right page. "So let's start with polynomials."

Emerson scooted in close again, and I tried to focus on the math problem at hand, not how close he was, his shoulder almost touching mine.

I took a deep breath. "And after this, we'll get started on your social studies project. I bet you could interview Mr. Roberts. I heard he's a vet. I bet he'd have plenty of really cool stuff to tell you—"

Emerson waved his hand at me. "Uh, Harper? Can I borrow a pencil first?"

"Emerson!" I whisper shouted. I pulled out my handy bag of pre-sharpened pencils and handed him one. "Here. Maybe that's the first thing we need to master. Showing up to class prepared."

He took the pencil, but his eyes didn't go back to the math notes in front of us. Instead, his eyes stayed on mine for a second too long, which had my stomach feeling kind of funny again.

I shoved that feeling down, down, down. This was strictly a peer-to-peer tutoring relationship.

Nothing more.

NINE

M r. Roberts did have lots to share with Emerson.

Emerson and I looked over the project rubric at lunch a few days later. We sat outside at some picnic tables, my lunch bag containing a turkey sandwich forgotten beside us.

I pointed to the requirements on the rubric with my pencil. "Okay, so we have to write down the definitions of primary source and secondary source and give an example of each," I said, looking up at him for a response.

The cool breeze made the sun bearable, and I liked the way it made Emerson's dark curls dance slightly.

"Where's your project?" he asked.

I opened my mouth, then spoke quickly. "Uh, I don't have it with me."

Emerson pressed his lips into a smile. "You already turned it in, didn't you?"

I scoffed. "No..." Even though I totally had.

Emerson covered his mouth, but the sound of his laugh reached me loud and clear.

I shoved him playfully and said, "You're the worst!"

My phone buzzed with a social media notification, and I noticed the time. "Time to focus. We only have a few minutes left before lunch is over."

He settled down.

"Definition of primary and secondary sources," I asked.

Emerson gave me a blank stare.

I gave him another second but nothing. "Mrs. Lee was just talking about this yesterday."

He crossed his arms in front of his chest. "I got nothin'."

I turned to him, swinging my leg outside the wooden bench. "Like Mr. Roberts' interview. Would you say that's a primary source or a secondary source?"

He shrugged, fidgeting with his pencil on the table. "Primary?"

I smiled. "Good. Yeah, it's primary. Do you know why, though?"

Another blank stare.

Once I explained the difference, he got it. "You understand this stuff," I said. "You just don't pay attention in class."

He finished writing his answers down. "I like the way you explain it. In class, I can't help but fall asleep.

It's like the teachers drone on and on forever on purpose."

I grabbed his notes on his interview with Mr. Roberts. "This is so cool. Mr. Roberts fought in Vietnam? I think Ms. Ellie was hardly a teenager at this time."

I kept on reading. "He saw his friend die in battle? That's so sad," I said, tearing up.

Glancing at Emerson for his reaction, I put the notes down. But all Emerson did was keep writing.

Ms. Ellie had told me all about watching the first moon landing on TV as a kid, but Mr. Roberts' story sounded intense.

I kept on reading. We were supposed to write a reflection about the interview and what we had learned from the experience.

Emerson's short paragraph was on the back. His handwriting was small but legible. So different from my large cursive lettering.

He'd written about what it must have been like to fight in a real war, how lucky we had it today, and what it meant that good people like Mr. Roberts had given so much.

I looked at Emerson, who was still writing about primary and secondary sources. "This is really good."

He hardly met my eyes before looking away. Then he shrugged. "I need at least a B on this dumb project."

I put the paper down and slid it toward him, wishing I could take a peek at what was really going on behind those dark eyes.

THE SOUND of keys turning the lock on the front door woke me from my latest Netflix binge. I opened my eyes to find my mom closing the door behind her and locking it again.

She faced me, purse hanging from her shoulder, eyes tired, and wisps of hair falling around her face. "Honey, I told you not to wait up for me. It's almost two in the morning."

I stretched and yawned. "I fell asleep hours ago. I promise. How was work?" I asked.

She landed on the couch beside me. Her purse fell to the floor, and she leaned back and closed her eyes. Twelve-hour shifts were our normal, but that didn't mean she didn't come home exhausted. "Brutal. Saturday nights always are, especially after the urgent care closes for the evening."

I gave her a hug as best as I could.

She put her arms around me. "But I'm glad to be home. Hey, you want some French toast in the morning? I think we have some strawberries. And then maybe a little shopping?"

I shrieked in excitement and clapped my hands to my mouth. "Really?" I tried to tone it down a notch. Maybe she meant window shopping, although any girl time together would be fun.

She smiled, the lines around her eyes creasing. They were my favorite thing about her. "Really. I think we have a little extra money left over this week, and I thought maybe we could buy a little something."

I screamed again and gave her another hug. I pulled away, too excited to sleep. She looked the same. "You want some ice cream?"

But I was already off the couch and headed toward the kitchen. I brought back two spoons and our favorite pint: mint chocolate chip.

I let her take the first bite. "Hmm," she said. "I needed that after the kind of day I had today."

She handed the little container over to me, and I took a big spoonful, savoring the mint chocolatey goodness.

Mom looked at me. "So how's school been going? I feel like I've hardly been around this week. I'm kind of glad you're not just home alone all day."

I exhaled. "It's good. I'm really enjoying the elective I have in the afternoon."

She nodded. "At the nursing home?"

"Yep," I replied. "I made a new friend. Her name is Ms. Ellie, and you'd love her. She's a hoot, Mom."

I told her about Ms. Ellie and everything she'd told me about growing up in the '60s and '70s. "And you know she went and saw Jaws, like, when it first came out? Isn't that crazy?"

Mom nodded slowly, a weird glaze in her eyes. Maybe it was time for bed. She took my hand. "I'm so proud of you, Harper. You're an amazing kid. You've handled the past year like a pro, with moving here, my new job, the long hours, and now summer school. So many kids would have pitched a fit about having to go, especially because of something silly like credits not transferring."

I blinked, pressing my lips into a smile. "Thanks, Mom," I said softly.

She brushed a strand of hair away from my eye. "So tell me more about summer school. Have you made any other friends? Maybe someone your age?" she teased.

I thought about that, giving her the pint of ice cream back. "Well, there are these three girls in my classes, but they're not really my friends…"

She dug around for some ice cream. "Are they not nice?"

I shook my head. "Not always."

"That's too bad. I know how hard it must be for you now that your friends are gone for the summer."

Emerson came to mind, and I spoke before really thinking. "Well, there is someone." I stopped, meeting her eyes for a second and then looking down. "I mean, he's not really a friend, I guess—"

My mom's crinkly smile eyes were back. "Is that so?"

I fidgeted with the blanket around my legs, shaking my head. "He's not really a friend. But he's in my classes, too, and he's the only other person assigned at the nursing home."

My mom set the ice cream container aside. "Does this boy have a name maybe?"

I fought the urge to giggle and look away. "Emerson. He's making up some classes too."

My mom nodded, and I could tell she wanted more details.

"I offered to help him with his homework and stuff. During our free time at the nursing home," I said. "He's smart. He just doesn't always apply himself. If he could, he'd just skateboard around all day, I'm sure."

My mom raised her eyebrows. "Skateboard, huh? Sounds like a bad boy," she teased.

"Kind of," I confessed. "But he has this other side too."

My mom got the same far-off look Ms. Ellie got when she remembered her younger years. Like she was looking at the ceiling but was actually replaying memories in her mind. "Goodness, bad boys were my weakness when I was your age." She looked at me. "How do you think I met your father? He wore this black leather jacket, rode around in a motorcycle. He got into a fight every other week." She seemed to come back down to earth. "It sure was fun while it lasted, even if he never did grow out of it."

Her phone buzzed, and she picked it up.

Meanwhile, I blinked several times and thought about everything she'd just said.

I tried to imagine what my mom and dad must have been like when they were my age. My mom had only been a few years older when she'd had me. They'd been together for a few years, but always on and off. Up until I was about ten.

She thought I didn't really know, but I remembered every single time my dad broke her heart. She'd say she was sick and lay in bed for a few days, hardly eating. I'd lay in bed with her, and we'd watch movies and order in.

My mom's voice jarred me out of my thoughts. "Goodness, it's super late. We should get to bed. Or we'll be having French toast for lunch."

She kissed me on the forehead.

"Yeah," I said, standing up.

A few minutes later, I lay in bed, still processing everything my mom had said earlier. As tired as I'd been just a few minutes ago, I just couldn't sleep.

My mom was right. Bad boys like Emerson were fun and cute, but they were far from the kind of guy I should be with. Not unless I wanted to end up heart-broken like her.

TEN

I continued helping Emerson with his homework and upcoming tests. But I closed off my heart to him.

When he asked me if I wanted to grab a bite after we finished our homework early during lunch, I held up my turkey sandwich and said no thanks.

"You've gotta have fun sometime, you know," he said, standing up and picking up his skateboard.

For me, fun was limited to eating popcorn on the couch and watching movies, shopping with my mom if I was lucky, or hanging out with my friends. It definitely couldn't include hanging out with Emerson.

Or letting my gaze linger on his mouth, his eyes, or his hands. Thinking about his slightly husky voice. Nope, nope, nope.

I pressed my lips into a half-hearted smile. "I'd hate to be late for class. It starts in twenty minutes."

He shrugged. "I don't know if I feel like sitting in a hard plastic chair for forty-five minutes today." He pretended to think really hard. "Yeah, no. I'm out." He hopped on his skateboard and rode a couple feet, leaning back and then forward. Letting his foot hit the pavement, he looked back at me. "You sure you don't want to come? I know this place with the best nachos."

I bit my lip, not daring to meet his eyes. "No, I can't. Thanks, though. Maybe some other time. " Like when it didn't mean skipping class, which I was physically incapable of doing. The school building pulled me in like a magnet during school hours, and there was nothing I could do about it. "Besides, how many times have you skipped? You're gonna risk not getting credit due to unexcused absences."

Emerson put his hands on his hips. "I'll be fine. I've only missed class a few times."

He looked like he wanted to say something else, but he didn't. Instead, he gave me a wave and rode away. When he got to the steps leading down to the parking lot, he jumped, his board landing on the thin metal rail. Then he hopped off at the bottom, still in one piece.

In no time at all, he was long gone.

I texted my friends, wondering what they were up to and missing them more than ever. Talking to them in the hallways in between classes or at lunch felt like forever ago, and all I wanted was to see them again.

But after fifteen minutes, no one responded. I wasn't surprised. They were probably busy doing all kinds of fun and exciting things while I was stuck here. With no one to talk to or laugh with.

Before lunch officially ended, I was already on my way back to class, hugging my books to my chest.

———

I WAS SURPRISED to see Emerson already at the nursing home when I arrived.

Usually, I got there first, but when I walked in, he was already strolling toward the elder day care wing, several daisies in his hand.

I caught up to him in the main room of the wing. "What's that?" I asked. I adored fresh flowers, and these looked hand-picked.

He took a second to answer. "I remembered some of the ladies saying they wished there were some flowers around here. So I brought some from my sister's garden."

Is that what he'd spent his extended lunch break doing? "You remembered that?" I asked with a wide smile. Ms. Ellie had requested fresh flowers to brighten up the place a few days ago, but Ms. Nancy had said it simply wasn't in the budget.

He opened his mouth, like he wasn't sure what to say. "My sister has a garden."

Like that was all the explanation that was needed. For Emerson, it was.

I touched one of the daisies with my fingers. "They're lovely. Ms. Ellie and the other ladies are going to love these."

A minute later, the daisies were in a purple vase, carefully arranged by a very happy Ms. Ellie.

Just watching her circle that vase and move each flower this was or that was a treat. She stepped back and admired her work. "It'd be even better if we had some baby's breath to accent them, but these daisies are exquisite, aren't they?"

I admired her work too. "They really are. You did a great job, by the way."

She clasped her hands together and beamed. "Just a little something I picked up over the years." Her eyes scanned the room, and I saw where they landed. Emerson was at his usual table with Mr. Roberts. Today they were working on a crossword puzzle together, one in the paper. Emerson jotted letters down while Mr. Roberts took charge of guessing the correct words.

"He's been wanting to do those crossword puzzles for ages, but his sight isn't what it used to be. And he hates fiddling with reading glasses," Ms. Ellie said.

I took in the sweet image of Emerson helping Mr. Roberts. "Emerson has a soft spot for him, doesn't he?" I said, thinking out loud.

Ms. Ellie nodded. "Sure does. That Emerson appears rough around the edges, but I can tell he has a big heart. Especially if he brought over these flowers." She winked at me. "A man who brings you flowers tends to be a keeper. Remember that, Harper."

I pretended not to understand her sly comment. She took a seat at a nearby table with some other ladies and began chatting up a storm.

Mrs. Porter stepped out of her office and came

right over. "These are some beautiful daisies. Did you bring them in?" she asked.

I shook my head. "Emerson did, actually."

She glanced over at him, and I took note of the clearly surprised look on her face. "That was kind of him. I always wanted to do little things like this for our residents, maybe a fun little event, but our budget just won't allow it."

"That's too bad," I said. Ms. Nancy told me that the nursing home relied on donations to stay open. The families of the residents were charged according to income, and really, it was a miracle they were even still open, mainly thanks to local business donations. "Maybe we could do a fundraiser sometime," I offered.

She gave me a tight-lipped smile. "Thank you, Harper. I wish we could, but we're stretched as it is, both with time and money. I can't ask Ms. Nancy to put in any more hours. A volunteer would have to do it."

Before I could say anything else, the phone in her office rang, the shrill noise reaching us all the way across the room. She took off, and I joined Ms. Ellie and her friends.

My eyes slid back to Emerson and Mr. Roberts. Except this time, he glanced my way, and our gazes met for a split second.

I looked away quickly, my heart skipping a couple beats.

Then I wondered how many people had gotten to see this other side of Emerson Lopez besides me.

ELEVEN

E merson and I stepped outside at the end of our shift at the nursing home.

Dark gray clouds crowded the sky for miles, and the wind blew my hair into my face. I tried and failed to get my long, blonde tresses under control. I must have looked ridiculous, but Emerson's gaze was up instead of on me. "I think it's going to start pouring any minute."

We crossed the street together and headed toward the school. Just as we were a few dozen feet away from the front doors, a siren went off.

I jumped, sure it had be firefighters or an ambulance nearby. But it was really loud.

Emerson's eyes met mine. "I think that's the tornado siren."

My mouth fell, but before I could say anything, a loud voice reached us. It was Ms. Moreau, waving us toward her from the front doors of the school building.

We jogged inside. She made sure the doors closed behind her and faced us. "Oh, I'm glad you two made it back just in time."

The siren kept going off in the background, but it wasn't nearly as loud as when we were outside.

We followed her to the girls' bathrooms down the hall. "I have to go check the rest of the building. You two go in there with the rest of the students. I'll be right back."

I touched Ms. Moreau's elbow. "Is there really a tornado?"

She exhaled. "I'm not sure. But everything's okay. We just have to take precautions. Just go in and get into position, like the drill from a few weeks ago."

With that, she was off, and Emerson led me into the girls' bathroom.

There was a handful of students in there already, all sitting with their backs against the wall and textbooks in their laps. The P.E. teacher, who I knew was Ella's boyfriend's dad, stood against one of the sinks. He nodded at us and scribbled something on his clipboard.

Emerson and I sat down, and my thoughts immediately went to my mom. Then the residents at the nursing home. Were they okay? Surely that old restored building couldn't stand up to a tornado.

With all sorts of scenarios in my head, I drew my knees up to my chest and wrapped my arms around them. I grabbed my phone out of my pocket and texted my mom.

The siren was still going strong, and with each

crescendo of the blaring sound, my breathing got a little faster.

I bit my lip, trying to stay calm. When I didn't get a reply back, I put my phone out of sight next to me.

Something brushed my fingers, and I realized it was Emerson's hand. "Are you okay?" he whispered.

I nodded quickly, not wanting to turn toward him.

His low voice reached my ear, and he squeezed my hand. "Hey, it's gonna be okay."

A couple of deep breaths later, the sound of the siren disappeared. I looked up at the P.E. teacher, and he checked his phone. He tapped a message out and then looked at us. "All clear. Head to the library and wait for dismissal."

Before he was even done with his last sentence, everyone was already up and heading toward the bathroom exit. Coach followed them, and Emerson and I trailed behind.

Back in the hallway, I shivered, glad that was over. My phone buzzed in my pocket, and I grabbed it. It was my mom.

Mom: I'm okay. Are you? Love you.

I tapped back a quick response, letting her know I was fine and still at school. Then I put my phone away.

Emerson hung back with me, and I found it impossible to look at him. "That was my mom," I said. "She's okay."

I glanced at him for half a second before facing forward again.

"Good," he said.

Trying to fill the silence, I said, "I guess it was just a false alarm."

We reached the library, and Emerson opened the door for me. I gave him a small smile and my eyes locked on his, hoping the awkward moment was over.

But the way he looked at me had me looking away again.

Maybe that siren had been a false alarm, but inside, my heart was still hammering, letting me know that what I felt for Emerson was far from false.

———

ONE OF MY favorite things about hanging out with older people was seeing how fun and rowdy they got around music.

Instead of arts and crafts, Ms. Nancy had done something special. She'd discovered Spotify and Pandora, and Ms. Ellie had convinced her to ditch arts and crafts for a dance session.

Most of the residents clapped and smiled and cheered from their tables, but a few of them got up and joined Ms. Ellie, moving to the top hits of the sixties and seventies. Two or three residents did what they did best: snore.

Ms. Ellie closed her eyes and swung her hips. "Oh, this song takes me back…"

She grabbed my hands, and I laughed, trying to copy her steps.

Emerson and Mr. Roberts smiled from their usual corner, and my cheeks burned. Mr. Roberts muttered something to Emerson, and Emerson chuckled, his smile wide and his eyes full of something I'd never really seen there before: joy.

Mr. Roberts stood up, and Emerson was there in a flash, making sure he was steady. Then Mr. Roberts made his way over to the dance floor, and I stopped to see what he was going to do. Maybe he was going to join in on the dancing.

But he went right over to Ms. Ellie, whose smile grew wider and wider the closer he got.

He stood in front of her, and my gaze met Emerson's just a few feet away before we both turned our attention back to Ms. Ellie and Mr. Roberts.

He extended his hand. "May I have this dance?"

As if on cue, the music turned to something slow and romantic, and I spun around to find Ms. Nancy at her computer with a knowing grin on her face and a glimmer in her eye.

I laughed out loud and took Mr. Roberts's seat so I could have a front-row view of the cutest thing I'd ever seen. Emerson sat down quietly next to me, but my eyes stayed glued to the old couple in front of us. I grabbed my phone and took a few pictures.

Mr. Roberts' hands lay at Ms. Ellie's waist, while her arms rested on his shoulders. They swayed slowly back and forth to the music, and Ms. Ellie closed her eyes. "It was about time," I heard her say.

My heart faltered. "They are precious," I said with a sigh.

"They are," Emerson said. "You know, his wife died like twenty years ago."

I frowned. "Ms. Ellie's second husband died several years ago too."

I couldn't imagine being lonely, without a partner in crime, for so long. They must have lived most of their lives with their spouses, just to lose them from one moment to the next. The one person they'd slept next to, eaten with, laughed with…now gone forever.

Everyone deserved somebody to hold during a dance. But especially ever-smiling Ms. Ellie and kind and quiet Mr. Roberts.

Emerson cleared his throat, and I glanced at him. He reached his hand toward me. "Shall we?" he said, biting his lip.

Unable to utter a single word, I answered his question by placing my hand in his. He led me to the middle of the room, next to Ms. Ellie and Mr. Roberts, and another cacophony of laughter, clapping, and cheering reached us. But just now, it felt kind of far away, like we were inside our own bubble and time ran a little slower in here.

Emerson put his hands on my hips, and I tried not to hyperventilate. I put my hands on his shoulders, and I realized I'd never really done this before. It was new, and I didn't know where to step or sway.

And it didn't help that Emerson was right there, his face—his mouth—just a few inches away.

He smiled. "It's okay. Just follow me. Listen to the music."

I tried to do that, but I wondered if I was still doing it all wrong. "You're good at this," I said with a smile. "I…have no idea what I'm doing."

Emerson's eyes, his smile, reassured me. He held me a little closer. "Just hang on to me. Follow my steps."

Glancing down at our feet, my strappy sandals and his royal blue sneakers, I did just that. I held onto Emerson, and we moved together to the sound of music. This way and that. He moved us in a slow circle around the room. I didn't want it to end, but of course, songs only lasted so long.

Our moment was over. We stepped away from each other, each of us looking away. Another song started, this time loud and fast and upbeat.

My gaze met Emerson's for a second. He shoved his hands in his pockets.

I found my voice. "Thanks for the dance."

He nodded. We found Ms. Ellie and Mr. Roberts making their way back to their seats, Ms. Ellie's arm in his.

When he sat down, she came over to me.

I beamed at her. "You were great! Where'd you learn to dance like that?"

She winked at me. "Ooh, I had a few different teachers. All handsome, of course."

I laughed.

She glanced back at Mr. Roberts. "I always did have a weakness for a handsome soldier, though."

We giggled like girls, and when the music stopped and Ms. Nancy called us to the movie room, we followed everyone else in.

Once I found my usual table, I got out my social

studies homework, but it was impossible to concentrate, even as I tried to help Emerson.

It didn't help that he was sitting so close, or that his lips called to me.

Then I noticed how his gaze stayed on me a little too long, and my heart responded by pounding even harder. And it definitely didn't help that I couldn't get the memory of his hands on my waist out of my mind.

TWELVE

E merson sat a few rows away in social studies, fidgeting with his pencil. He glanced my way and showed me his worksheet. Half the answers were missing.

I shook my head.

Help, he mouthed.

The bell would ring any minute. I finished writing the last sentence on my own worksheet and put my pencil down. The less homework I had tonight, the more time I'd have to chat with my friends and watch a movie. Maybe play with the new makeup I'd bought over Fourth of July weekend.

I tried to mouth something back to Emerson, but the bell rang.

He walked right over. "Remind me why I should care about this again."

I stood up. "Because it'll help you do well on the test and pass the class. So you can graduate." And avoid juvenile detention. "Come on, we'll work on it at the nursing home. It's not that bad. I promise."

He scoffed. "You promise?"

Emerson followed me out of class, and I ignored the pointed looks from Becca and her friends. Lately, Emerson and I had been talking more and more during class. Working together when the teacher allowed group work or saying hello in the mornings.

It must have been odd to everyone, seeing as how Emerson didn't usually say hi to anyone.

And he was turning in most of his work, mostly because I wouldn't stop nagging him—in a gentle way, of course—until he did. And studying. At the nursing home anyway. No one had been more surprised than Mr. Nguyen when Emerson had earned a B on the latest quiz.

Emerson had shown me his paper right away. "At this rate, I might actually pass."

"I told you you could do it," I said. "Showing up is 80 percent of getting a B."

We made our way to the nursing home together. Up ahead, Ms. Moreau stepped out of her office. I liked the eighties vibe she had going on with the fanny pack she wore around her waist and the high-waisted jeans. Her pristine white sneakers and pastel-colored t-shirt finished off the look perfectly.

Her eyes met mine, and she smiled.

I smiled back.

"Emerson, Harper, I was hoping to catch you two. Can I see you for a minute?" she asked.

We followed her into her office, and she closed the

door. We sat down in front of her desk, and she walked around to her own seat. "I won't take up too much of your time. I know they must be waiting for you back at the nursing home. But since I'm the student advisor for your elective, I wanted to take a few minutes to check in." She rested her hands on her desk. "So how is everything going so far?"

Emerson and I glanced at each other.

I turned back to Ms. Moreau. "Really good. I'm having a lot of fun volunteering."

Ms. Moreau directed her gaze at Emerson, who shrugged. "I like it."

Ms. Moreau nodded. "Good. Mrs. Porter tells me you two are doing great with attendance, with the exception of a few absences." She gave a discreet smile to Emerson who looked down. "But attendance has been pretty much perfect recently, which is excellent. I'm glad you two are enjoying your time there. I know they've been grateful for the help."

She paused for a moment, and I wondered if that was it.

But she looked up at us again. "I also wanted to let you know that there will be a final for this elective. The majority of your grade will come from attendance and a general evaluation from Ms. Nancy. You two seem to be doing fine there. But to receive full credit for the class, you'll also be required to turn in a final project within a month's time."

I sat up. "What kind of project?" I asked, ready to be handed a rubric of some sort. I could handle rubrics. But none came.

Ms. Moreau smiled. "You get to create your own project. Doesn't that sound like fun?"

I glanced at Emerson again, whose expression didn't really look like he was having fun. More like he was holding back a huge groan.

"You can work together or individually, it's up to you. But I want you to think of some kind of project that will involve the community and involve the nursing home. Your proposal for this project is due in a week. After that, the project, your report of how it all went, and what you learned will be due at the end of the month. On your last day."

She finally handed each off us a sheet of paper, outlining most of what she had just said.

I read over it. "So it's 20 percent of our grade?"

She nodded. "Be as creative as you like. The sky's the limit."

A minute later, we grabbed our stuff and left her office. I read the paper over again, Emerson walking next to me. "Well, this should be fun," I said with a nervous smile. "It can't be that bad, right?"

Emerson stuffed the paper into his backpack, and I had a feeling it would end up in a crumpled mess at the very bottom. "Are you kidding? I'd rather take a test. And that's saying something. I hate stuff like this."

"Come on, it'll be fun." Without even thinking I grabbed his hand. Then I dropped it, fast, and we kept walking. Emerson didn't say a word, and all I could do was focus on not hyperventilating out of sheer embarrassment. What was I thinking?

I could not do that again.

———

IT WAS SATURDAY EVENING, and after having dinner with my mom a few blocks away from home, she got up to leave.

She kissed me on the forehead. "Are you sure you're okay taking the bus home?"

I nodded. "Definitely. It's only a few minutes. I'll text you when I'm there."

She gave me a soft smile. "Okay, then. Don't miss it. You know the bus stops running soon." She gave me a hug. "Hopefully we can get you a car next year. Promise."

Between weekend babysitting gigs here and there and my mom putting half of my allowance toward my first car fund, it would definitely wouldn't happen until well into senior year. But I was okay with that. I didn't mind walking or taking the bus at all.

With one final wave, my mom headed off to work, and I finished eating my small ice cream cone.

It was still pretty early, so I decided to do some window shopping and walk off the sugar in my system. Maybe it was the brownie or the fact that it was the perfect summer night, but I was in a great mood.

I stepped outside and observed the sun in the distance, hiding behind the tree line. This was my favorite time of day because of the sky. It burned red and purple and orange and every hue in between.

And I was perfectly comfortable in my jean shorts and sleeveless, flowy shirt.

I only wished I had someone to share this evening with. But it was fun all the same.

Making my way down the block, I took in all the shops, the clothes, the shoes, all calling to me. But it wasn't meant to be. Not tonight anyway. So I walked toward the park instead. The bus stop was there.

Since the sun was tucked away for the night, I probably should be too.

Once I arrived at the bus stop, the sound of a skateboard caught my attention. It was hard to see in the ever-growing dark, but someone was there.

I made my way toward the playground through the parking lot. A couple of families with screaming toddlers walked past me, clearly ready to get home.

I stopped at the swings and sat down on one. Just like I had suspected, Emerson was a few dozen feet away by the picnic tables.

Slowly swinging, I watched him for a few minutes. What I loved about Emerson on a skateboard was that he never stood still. He had so much energy, jumping over tables and doing backflips with his skateboard in hand.

It was mesmerizing to watch, and I only wished I was at talented as Emerson at something. But I didn't want to interrupt him. Even though he was practicing in public, this felt like something private.

The sky became darker, and I knew it was time to go. The bus would be here any minute, and at this time, it only ran every half hour.

I got up quietly and began making my way back to the bench in front of the bus stop.

But the sound of Emerson's voice made me freeze. "You sit there and watch me for ten minutes, but you won't say hi?"

Exhaling slowly, I turned around to face him. All of a sudden, I was thankful that it was dark and the lights from the shop and the street didn't quite reach us. Only a single corner light illuminated our faces, but it wasn't enough to let him see the look of horror on my face.

I had to say something. "Hi. Sorry."

Emerson came closer, his skateboard tucked under his arm. "Why are you apologizing? I was just teasing you."

I took him in, from messy hair to black t-shirt and worn blue jeans. Fidgeting with my hair, I said, "I didn't want to bother you. I was just...admiring your skateboarding."

Realizing how that sounded, I tried not to cringe.

He took another step toward me. "Thanks."

Glancing back toward the bus stop and making sure I wasn't missing my ride home, I said, "Have you always been that good?"

He smiled wide and laughed like he was remembering something. "Definitely not."

I couldn't help but smile back. "Really? I can't even imagine riding that thing on two feet on level pavement, much less on my hands or down the stairs. I'd break my neck so fast."

That made him laugh even harder. "It's not as hard as it looks."

"You promise?" I teased.

He blinked, his smile turning a little serious. "I promise."

I bit my lip and looked away, unable to keep my eyes locked with his a second longer. I willed my heart to stop beating so fast and for my stomach to stop doing somersaults inside me.

But they wouldn't listen.

"Here," Emerson said, holding out his hand. "I'll teach you."

I shook my head frantically. "No. No way. I can't—"

But he took my hand anyway.

"Emerson, I'm gonna fall and end up in the hospital—"

He laughed. "You'll be fine. I've got you."

My stomach did another backflip. Meanwhile, Emerson put down his skateboard in front of me. That small rectangular piece of plastic—or whatever it was—scared me. I was not good at things like balance or anything like that.

"No," I said, still shaking my head. I took a few steps back. "You do it first."

Mostly, I hoped he'd forget to make me do whatever he was going to do.

Especially when I saw him jog toward his skateboard and just hop on, gliding down the concrete.

How was he doing that?

He came back in my direction. "It's easy." He got

off the skateboard again, leaving only one foot on the board. "You use your other foot to start moving." Keeping his one foot steady and pushing off the ground with the other, he began skating away again. "Then you just put your foot on the board and kind of turn." Now he was sideways on his board somehow, and I still knew that there was no way I'd ever be able to do that.

He stopped in front of me with an evil grin. "Your turn, Harper."

Hearing my name come out of his mouth almost took away the fear of landing on my face.

Almost.

I kept shaking my head, at a loss for words.

He took my hand again. "I'll hold your hand while you push off. Just push off like three times. I promise you'll get it in no time."

"Emerson, you don't understand—"

"You can do this," he assured me. "I won't let you fall."

Even though I tried to get away, my left foot was already on the board. Emerson held on to my hand, tight, and I realized he wasn't going to let this go until I at least tried.

I met his gaze. "You better not let me fall."

He fell silent for a second. "Don't you trust me? How could I let you fall?"

And with that, I looked at the ground again, trying not to freak out over what he'd just said. I had to concentrate, seeing as how I was about to make a fool of myself.

I pushed off once, twice, and the board moved, bringing me along with it. But my other foot remained on the ground.

"Good," Emerson said. "Keep doing that. Then put both feet on the board. I'll keep holding your hand."

So I did, still terrified but also a teeny bit excited that I hadn't broken my face just yet.

I pushed off again, once, twice, three times. Then my right foot was on the board.

I shrieked, half in terror and half in disbelief. Emerson held on, moving alongside me.

My stance was all wrong, but my feet were off the ground. Then the board came to a standstill.

"Keep going," he said, still holding on to me. "This time, try to turn your feet once they're both on the board."

Again. Push, push, push, glide. I kind of did it, and this time, when I yelled, it was purely from how much fun I was having.

We ended up on the grass, and I stepped off.

Emerson held my hand for another second or two, even though I was no longer on his skateboard. "Told you you could do it," he said.

He was standing really close to me, my fingers intertwined in his, and I had to remember to breathe. The cool breeze made my skin erupt in goosebumps. Or maybe it was the way Emerson was looking at me right now.

The only sound I was aware of was my heart and

his breath. My eyes locked on his lips, and I felt like I was frozen with him in this moment.

His mouth was close, so close.

Then a loud familiar sound reached my brain, and I snapped out of it.

I spun around.

The bus. It was pulling away. There was no way I could catch up.

"Oh no," I said. "I missed it."

I turned back to Emerson for a second, and then we watched the bus turn around the corner and disappear.

"That was my ride home," I said.

My phone buzzed in my pocket. There were a few texts from my mom, wondering if I was home yet.

I texted her that I was on my way, that I had walked around the square.

"Is it far?" Emerson asked.

I looked up at him. "Twenty-minute walk." I told him where I lived. "And I think that was the last bus of the night." I sighed, wishing I had been paying more attention. I should have just stayed on the bench, as fun as it'd been to hang out with Emerson.

He picked up his board. "I'll walk you."

"Where do you live?" I asked.

Maybe he was heading home too.

"Off of Connor Road," he said.

I thought about that. "Isn't that in the opposite direction?"

He shrugged, holding up his board. "It won't take me very long to get home if I have this."

"Are you sure?" I asked. It'd be nice to have someone walk me home. Otherwise, I'd have to call a cab or my mom or something. Our town didn't have Uber yet.

He gave me a smile. "I don't mind at all. Come on."

THIRTEEN

E merson and I walked toward my house. A car passed us by here and there, and the only light came from the street lamps or those from businesses or houses.

The farther we got from downtown, the less businesses we passed and the more apartment complexes and houses popped up.

The more I thought about it, the more I decided that it was a good thing I had missed the bus. Now we could talk about our project. "So I was thinking," I began, "that maybe we could do some kind of fundraiser like the P.E. class is doing."

Emerson gave a "hmm."

"They're doing a car wash or something. What if we did something like that but more of a dance thing?"

That got his attention. "A dance thing? You realize there's only two of us, right?"

I nudged his shoulder. "Duh. I was thinking we

could make it a community event. Invite the whole town. Back in Wisconsin, people would do dollar dances sometimes."

Emerson lifted an eyebrow. "Dollar dance? And you're from Wisconsin? So does that mean you lived on a farm or something?"

I nudged into him a little harder this time. "No, I didn't live on a farm," I said with a laugh. "I don't know how to milk cows either."

Emerson smiled. "Really? Because I was trying to picture you milking a cow or feeding chickens or something."

"You're impossible," I replied. "But anyway, we can do a dollar dance. Members of the community can donate a dollar or however much they want to dance with a senior citizen. Or one of us. We'll have safety pins available so people can pin their donations to us. What do you think?"

He exhaled loudly. "I don't know, Harper. Are you sure you want to charge people to dance with you when you've got those two left feet?"

My mouth fell open, but I smiled, knowing he was teasing. "Okay, Mr. Dancing Expert. Just because you can waltz or whatever."

He smiled kind of sheepishly. "Actually, I don't just know how to waltz."

I stopped, and he stopped too. "So you do all these skateboard tricks—"

"It's called parkour," he said. "Skateboard parkour."

Once again, I felt speechless. "Skateboard parkour?"

I wasn't even sure what that meant, but really, I was just impressed with how much he could do. Meanwhile, my talent was watching Netflix movies on repeat and making the perfect batch of popcorn.

"But yeah. I can dance. My older sister loves to dance, and she would always make me be her partner." He shrugged again. "So I got good at it."

"Same sister who has a garden?" I asked. I'd only heard about his brothers.

He nodded, and we continued walking. "She's the oldest of all of us. She has a baby that's a year old. But she's a single mom."

"Wow," I said, trying to picture him dancing as a kid. "So what kind of dancing can you do? My mom can't dance to save her life, so I never picked it up either."

He looked down at the ground as he talked. Which was too bad because the night sky was so much better to look at. "All kinds of stuff, but mostly Spanish stuff."

That made me think of Dancing with the Stars. "Like salsa and mamba and stuff like that?" I asked, way too excited.

He laughed. "Salsa, sure. But there's way more kinds of music in my world than that."

I was curious what he meant by that. "Maybe we can play some of it at our fundraiser," I said. "If you can come up with a great playlist, English and Spanish, I bet it'll be a huge hit. We can draw both communities."

"Okay," he said. "My brother has a sound system we could borrow too. I can set it up and DJ."

"You'd do that?" I said.

"Sure," he said, but something in his eyes told me there was more to it than that.

I beamed up at him. "This is going to be so much fun. Just promise me one thing," I said, before I could completely chicken out.

"Name it," he said.

"Save a dance for me?" I breathed. "I mean, so you can teach me…"

What else was I going to say? My mind went blank, and he smiled.

"Count on it," he said.

We were quiet after that, but it wasn't long before we reached my house.

"This is me," I said as we walked up my driveway.

We stopped at my front door, and I checked the time on my phone. It was late.

"Thanks again for walking me home," I said.

Emerson was so close. All he had to do was move slightly to accidentally nudge me with his skateboard. "No problem," he said.

While he didn't always smile, I liked that I could usually find one in his eyes.

I dug my keys out of my pocket and unlocked my front door. But I didn't want to go inside.

With his free hand, he brushed my fingers. "Good night, Harper."

"Good night," I said softly.

And with that, Emerson stepped off the front step. With his skateboard landing at his feet, he jumped on and rode off into the cool night.

I watched him go, wishing our walk hadn't ended quite so soon.

———

ON MONDAY, Emerson found me at our usual picnic table outside. We hadn't said we'd be meeting up today, so I was surprised when he sat down next to me.

With a huge bite of turkey sandwich in my mouth, I turned away, focusing on swallowing my lunch without choking.

He slapped a paper down in front of me. "What'd you get on the math midterm?"

Taking a quick swig of water, I grabbed the sheet. "A B. Why?" It was his midterm in my hands, covered in red marks.

"As you can see, I definitely didn't get a B," he said.

He'd gotten a D. But he'd been so close to passing. "You only needed five more points to pass," I said.

He nodded. "Yeah, I hate these stupid tests. I forget everything we studied. Mr. Nguyen said I need at least a C+ on the final to pass the class. Plus keep turning in homework and stuff."

I turned to him. "We can study together for the

final again. I bet this will help. Mr. Nguyen usually puts a few of the same problems on the final."

Our math homework for tonight included fixing the mistakes we'd made on the mid-term, so we spent the rest of our lunch period doing just that.

I wasn't a math genius like Ella, though, so I struggled to fix my own mistakes. After a while, there was one equation neither of us could get the hang of.

"I don't get it," I said. "Why are we still not getting the right answer?"

Emerson groaned. "I hate math."

An idea came to mind. "Well, we're not giving up yet. I know someone who can help."

Emerson put his pencil down. "Tell me we're not asking Mr. Nguyen for help. The way he explains it only makes it worse."

I smiled. "Don't worry. She's not a math teacher, but she may as well be." I pulled my phone out of my pocket and texted Ella a picture of the math problem in question.

Harper: HELPPPP

Emerson read the text message over my shoulder. Three little dots appeared on my screen. I wasn't sure if I should exhale in relief or get my crazy beating heart to calm down due to the fact that Emerson had scooted in close.

"Who's Ella?" he asked.

I faced him for a half a second but immediately turned back to my phone. No way could I stand his face being so close to mine without stuttering or forgetting what my name was. "She's one of my best friends, and she's super smart when it comes to anything math or computer-related. She's half the reason I got an A in math last semester. Usually, I'm happy to get a B."

Emerson nodded, impressed. Then my phone dinged with a new message. Ella had sent me a picture of the math problem step by step.

Harper: THANKS! You're the best :)

Ella sent me back a nerd emoji.

Ella: Got any more of those math problems?

Emerson chuckled. "Here. Send her a picture of my midterm."

I nudged him playfully and laughed. "You are too much."

There was an odd look on his face, one that made my breath hitch and my heart practically jump out of my rib cage. Emerson had turned his body so he was completely facing my direction, one arm on the table.

It would have been so easy to just lean in and kiss him, but I couldn't. Nope, nope, nope. I could not do that.

Another part of me asked why not.

But no, we were just friends. I was just helping him out with summer school. In a month, it would be over, the regular school year would start, and everything would go back to the way it was before.

Emerson being the resident bad boy everyone avoided. Hanging out with my friends during lunch. Not Emerson.

Plus he didn't do relationships.

With all those reasons firmly in mind, I put my

phone down and picked up my pencil. "Okay, let's do this."

Emerson turned his body so that both his legs went back under the table. "Okay."

And we went back to doing math, just math. Even though I wanted to let my gaze linger on him, I didn't. Like he sensed what I was feeling, Emerson became all business too.

Before we could finish all the problems on his mid-term, he stood up. Hardly looking at me, he said, "I have to go."

I blinked up at him. "But we've got to head to the nursing home in like five minutes."

He picked up his skateboard. "There's something I've got to do." And without a second look toward me, he left, gone before I could say anything else.

FOURTEEN

That evening, I sat at home, alone and bored. My mom was working another midnight shift, and I'd finished my homework hours ago.

Dinner had been me eating leftovers in front of the TV. And for some reason, watching *To All The Boys* for the umpteenth time didn't have the same appeal anymore.

Maybe because I couldn't get my mind off of Emerson. He hadn't shown up to the nursing home today, and I wondered if he was upset with me.

Part of it didn't make sense because supposedly, he didn't do relationships. He preferred being by himself, and from what I'd seen last semester, that had been true.

But was it still? What else explained those moments we had? Did he really feel something for me? Or was I just a game to him?

My heart deflated at the thought of that.

My head told me letting myself get carried away around him wasn't a good idea.

I wouldn't be the first girl whose heart he broke. Trying to make things work with a bad boy hadn't gone so well for my mom. That was probably what scared me the most. I loved my mom, but I didn't want to be in her same shoes one day.

At some point, I wanted to find a guy who'd want to be with me for the long run. I knew that wouldn't come for a while yet, but I also didn't want to give any part of myself to someone who wasn't interested in being with me even as a boyfriend.

I ignored the buzzing coming from my phone and sat down on the sofa. My eyes closed on their own. I could check my notifications later. My breathing slowed. I just wanted to forget about everything and take a nap. Maybe go to bed, even though dinner had only been an hour ago. I wasn't in the mood to do anything.

Then my phone buzzed without stopping. I opened my eyes. It was a #BFF video chat. Turning on the lamp beside me so my friends could actually see me, I answered the call.

Lena smiled back at me along with Ella.

Then Rey appeared with a wave and finally Tori.

They immediately said hi and exclaimed about Lena's super tanned look. And Tori's cute top.

I just smiled and listened, glad to hear their voices.

Then Ella said, "Harper, you're being quiet tonight."

They all quieted down, and I sat up. "Sorry, guys. I guess I'm tired."

Tori leaned into the screen. Tonight, she was donning a high ponytail and bow, like she'd just finished cheer practice. "Well, tell us how summer school is going."

I shrugged. "I'm sure it's not as exciting as what you guys are doing."

I smiled as I said it, but I could feel the pity party just beginning. What was wrong with me? I didn't usually feel like this. I blinked hard and cleared my throat, but my voice quivered anyway. "Sorry, I just miss you guys."

Everybody's grins turned down, and guilt consumed me for turning this happy chat into a consolation party.

Rey said, "We miss you, too, Harp. You don't know how bad I wish I was home. This trip has already worn me out."

Ella nodded. "We'll be home before you know it. Just a couple more weeks."

It was more like a month, but all I did was nod. "You're right. It's just that my mom is working all the time, and there's nothing to do."

Tori spoke up. "How's everything going at the nursing home? I thought that was fun."

"It is," I said. "I think I'm just in a weird funk right now."

Lena stared back at me. "Just hang in there, girl. My family is talking about heading home early. My siblings and I have been telling them non-stop that we want a couple of weeks at home to settle in before school starts. I hate coming home the weekend before."

Ella smiled. "That's a great idea."

Tori coughed, and then she was on screen. "Are you sure that's all that's going on, Harp? You know you can tell us anything, right?"

I opened my mouth, not sure how to answer that. "Well…"

Lena came in close. "Is it boy trouble?"

I bit my lip. "Nothing's really happened. It's just…"

"Emerson?" Ella asked.

I nodded. "Not that hard to guess, huh?"

Tori smiled. "We saw the way you looked at him."

Rey nodded. "It sure seems like he's the only guy you've crushed on since you moved here."

Lena's mouth turned down. "He didn't try something on you, did he?"

I shook my head right away. "No, nothing like that."

Tori said, "Then what is it?"

Sighing, I said, "Sometimes I think we could be more than friends."

Lena raised her eyebrows. "I didn't even realize you guys were friends."

I shrugged. "It just happened, I guess. With volunteering at the nursing home. And having classes together. He actually seems kind of nice. You guys should see the way he helps Mr. Roberts. It's the sweetest thing ever."

Ella smiled. "Now, why didn't you tell us any of this before, huh?"

"I guess I knew you guys didn't think it was a good idea, me falling for a guy like Emerson. Maybe that's why I'm kind of in a funk. I know he doesn't have a great reputation, but sometimes I wonder if…"

The girls nodded even though I didn't finish my sentence. With them, I didn't have to.

Tori sighed. "That's the thing, Harp. You just won't know unless you try."

Lena added, "But trying could mean having an amazing boyfriend or getting your heart broken."

Ella and Rey grimaced a little at her words, and I probably did too. "I know," I said. "I wish I didn't feel this way, and who knows if he even feels the same…"

Tori said aloud what we were all thinking. "Does he feel the same way about you?"

I told them about the other night at the park, about our slow dance, and with each and every detail, the #BFFs looked more surprised and just listened.

Ella rested her cheek on her hand. "That is so romantic," she said.

Rey agreed, and so did Tori. But Lena looked less convinced.

"I'm happy for you, Harp," she said. "Just be careful, okay? No matter what. Maybe this is the real deal, and I hope it is. But just…be careful."

BUT I ALREADY HAD IT bad for Emerson.

That was the thing.

So I tried to stay away, keep things as emotionally distant as possible.

I helped him with homework, and we studied together for the upcoming final exams. We worked on our community project at the nursing home and volunteered together.

But I didn't let myself take in the way he smiled with Mr. Roberts or memorize the shape of his mouth, his shoulders, or what he sounded like.

I wasn't sure if he noticed, but maybe he did because he eventually started doing the same.

He smiled less when we were together, stopped sitting so close, and stopped saying goodbye after we were done volunteering.

All of it broke my heart.

We'd never shared a single kiss, yet Emerson Lopez had still managed to break my heart.

Ms. Ellie must have noticed I was unusually quiet recently because one afternoon, she said, "What is it, darling? Something's on your mind."

I looked up at her, an automatic smile on my face. Even though it didn't nearly reach my eyes, I hoped she'd just let it go. "Nothing," I said. "Just a little sad that summer is coming to an end. That's all. It's my favorite season."

But this summer had turned out to be not so great, with my friends gone and a doomed crush on a boy.

All Ms. Ellie said was, "Hmm." And we went back

to working on our puzzle. It was close to being finished.

Each day we'd gotten closer and closer to completing the picture. It was of Paris at sunset, and we were almost done revealing the Eiffel Tower in the background, with a completed bridge on one side and a beautiful river on the other. The sky had all the oranges and yellows and pinks that I loved.

"You know what my biggest regrets in life have been?" Ms. Ellie asked all of a sudden.

That super personal question had me looking up at her, the dozens of tiny little puzzle pieces forgotten on the table in front of me.

She didn't wait for me to respond. "Not telling someone how I really felt before it was too late."

Then she didn't say anything. Only our eyes talked, and I knew what she meant and that she knew that I knew what she meant.

I tried to go back to the puzzle, but she kept talking. "Love is a beautiful thing, Harper. The most beautiful thing life has to offer. It comes in so many forms. The important thing is that we don't let it slip by."

Just like that, my eyes slid to Emerson, who sat quiet and serious with Mr. Roberts. Was it me or did he look a little more serious than usual?

Maybe he didn't like that our time at the nursing home was soon coming to an end.

But I knew it was more than that. We'd be able to come back and see Ms. Ellie and Mr. Roberts if we really wanted to.

Ms. Ellie's voice reached my ears again, but I found it impossible to tear my eyes off of Emerson. "Love hurts sometimes, Harper. But you'd be surprised how much more often things end up working way better than you could have ever imagined."

What had Tori said? I'd never know unless I tried.

Did I dare let Emerson know how I felt about him?

My heart beat a little faster just at the thought.

I had no idea.

FIFTEEN

My mom poked her head into my room. "Are you sure you've got everything packed? Passport, phone charger, makeup, work from school?" she asked.

She had just gotten home from work, and instead of lounging around on the sofa today, I had to pack my things.

"I have everything," I said. "Don't worry."

"Two weeks is two weeks," she said, walking away. "I don't want you to forget anything important."

My two weeks with my dad started tomorrow. Instead of going to school, I'd be getting on a plane early in the morning and arriving back in Wisconsin by lunch. I was going to miss my mom like crazy, but at least this would be my own little adventure.

And maybe I'd finally get Emerson out of my head once and for all.

The whole emotionally distant thing was not

really working. Not when he was so physically close to me almost every day.

I just needed my feelings for him to disappear because I definitely wasn't brave enough to tell him how I really felt and then risk him saying he wasn't interested in me. Not for more than a summer fling.

My heart wouldn't survive that.

I'd hardly mentioned that I'd be gone for the next couple weeks. Just that I was going to see my dad, and that I wouldn't be back until the end of summer. That was it.

He'd barely nodded.

After double-checking my packing list, I stood back and admired all my hard work. It wasn't even dinner time, and my suitcase was packed and ready to go. My mom had already asked for the morning off so she could drop me off at the airport a couple hours away.

We'd have breakfast together before I left. I missed her already, even though she was downstairs finishing up dinner.

Most girls probably cringed at the thought of spending more time with their mom, but I hardly got to see mine, so I was glad we were going to have dinner together tonight.

When I walked downstairs, I smelled my favorite meal. "Oh, Mom, you shouldn't have."

But she had. The oven went off, and she put on her oven mitts and pulled out pot roast with potatoes, carrots, and tons of veggies. There was corn on the cob and a Caesar salad and hand-squeezed lemonade.

While she gathered everything at the dinner table, I set out plates and silverware and lit some candles.

"Mom, you outdid yourself," I said as we sat down at the table.

She beamed. It wasn't often that she cooked like this. "Well, thank you."

I loaded my plate with everything, and I dug in. The pot roast practically melted in my mouth. "Hmm, my compliments to the chef," I said, dabbing at my mouth with a napkin.

Before my mom could say anything, her phone went off in the living room. "Sorry, sorry. I forgot to turn that off."

She got up and left.

We didn't do special candle-lit dinners like this very often with her work schedule and our tight budget, but when we did, we went all out. Dressing up, turning our phones off, and really catching up.

So I was surprised to hear her voice coming from the living room. She'd only answer if it was an emergency. Maybe she had to go into work?

I bit my lip and hoped not. I set my fork and knife down, not wanting to continue dinner by myself.

A few minutes later, she walked back in, disappointment clear on her face. "Honey, I'm so sorry."

I blinked back up at her. "What is it? Do you have to go in to work?"

Maybe having a full twenty-four hours off had been too good to be true.

She sat down next to me. "It wasn't work, sweetie.

It was your dad. He says he won't be able to have you for the next couple of weeks after all."

She went on to say something about a work trip, a chance for some extra money, but I hardly heard any of it.

I hadn't realized how much I'd been looking forward to this trip until now.

My dad and I had never been super close, but this was my chance to go back to Wisconsin, to fly for the first time, to maybe have an adventure of my own this summer.

And just like that, it was all gone.

Gone because my dad decided something else was more important than the two weeks he got out of the year to spend time with me.

My mom's voice broke through the turmoil of my thoughts. "Honey, Harper? Are you okay?"

I looked at her and nodded. "Yeah, I'm fine. It's fine. Now I don't have to miss school."

Her eyes studied me, and I made sure to turn my mouth up into a careful smile and push the tears back.

"Are you sure you're okay? I know you were looking forward to this," she said.

I nodded quickly and stared down at my full plate of food. Unlike a few minutes ago, my appetite was now completely gone. I stood up. "I'm going to go unpack, if you don't mind. I'll finish this later."

Without a second look back, I sped off to my room. Once I shut the door quietly behind me, I sank down to the floor, and that's when the tears came.

———

AFTER I'D SHOVED my still-packed suitcase in my closet last night, I'd somehow crawled into bed. I must have fallen asleep pretty quickly because that was all I remembered.

At some point, my mom must have come in and laid down beside me because sometime around dawn, I'd felt her wake up and go. She hadn't done that since I was little kid, although back then, it was usually me crawling into her bed in the middle of the night.

I could have gotten up and wished her a nice day before she left, maybe started a pot of coffee, but instead, I'd pretended to be asleep until I heard her car leave the driveway.

My mom was supposed to have the morning off, but she must have gotten called in. Part of me was sad we didn't have our planned breakfast—or our planned dinner—but I also knew we could use any overtime she could get at the hospital.

It was okay, I told myself. I'd have the rest of summer to hang out with her. As for my dad, well, he had more important things to do, and I would have been lying to myself if I thought it didn't sting.

It did.

I lay in bed until I had twenty minutes left to get ready for school and eat something before I had to go too.

I settled for a quick cup of coffee, not really in the

mood to eat. Instead of falling in nice long, styled waves, my hair was up in a ponytail today, and I only had on minimal makeup.

I couldn't wait to get today over with so I could come home and tether myself to the couch. Nothing some caramel popcorn and a good Netflix rom-com couldn't fix.

Or at least help me forget.

But the closer I got to school, the more it hurt.

When I walked into math late and saw Emerson's surprised look, it hurt even worse somehow.

I took a seat as far away from Emerson as I could, and I lay my head down on my desk, hoping my cardigan sleeve soaked up the tears.

My friends would hardly recognize me if they could see me right now. Ever smiling, good girl Harper, crying in class.

I missed my friends more than ever.

As Mr. Nguyen handed out tonight's homework, I opened up our messages thread and typed out a quick text.

Harper: Not headed to Wisconsin after all. Didn't work out. Miss you guys.

My phone buzzed only seconds later with an influx of sorry's and sad emojis.

I typed out one more message, swallowing the lump in my throat.

Harper: No worries :) I'm glad I'll be here when you guys get back. Plus more time I'll get to spend home with my mom.

The bell rang, and even though it was time for social studies, I left math and turned the other way.

Maybe I was the good girl to the rest of my friends, but today, I was taking a page out of Emerson's book.

SIXTEEN

I've never skipped class before. Not here, not back in Wisconsin.

It felt completely odd to me, not being where I was supposed to be, doing something that was against the rules.

I walked out of school near the gym and found a large tree. I sat down, resting my back against the rough bark and stared up at the mid-morning sky. The sun grew hotter by the minute, so I shrugged off my cardigan. Then I closed my eyes and exhaled.

This should have been my summer. Napping in the warmth of the sun and relaxing with a good swim.

For a few minutes, I let myself stretch out and forget where I was.

Until I heard soft steps in the grass. I sat straight up and opened my eyes. "What are you doing here?" I asked.

Emerson stood before me, his skateboard under

his arm. "May I?" he asked, nodding at the spot in the grass next to me.

Not knowing how else to respond, I nodded, and he took a seat, laying his board a few feet away. "As your fellow peer, I was concerned when I didn't see you in class a few minutes ago. I'd hate for your grades to slip due to poor attendance."

Shielding the sun with my eyes, a smile grew on my face. "Is that so?" I asked.

He nodded. "Oh yeah."

After a moment, no one said anything, and I remembered that talking to him like this, letting my guard down, probably wasn't the best idea. Not if I was going to get over him.

Just as I opened my mouth to say we should get to class, he said, "Is there a reason you decided to bail today? Is it the same reason you're obviously not on a plane right now?"

Wow, just like that, he'd gone and addressed the elephant in the room.

I stuttered for a few seconds. "Uh, um, I—things didn't work out. And I'm not going," was all I managed to say.

Probably seeing the pained look on my face, he quietly said, "I'm sorry."

I gave him a quick smile. "It's okay. Probably for the best."

And once again, the same feelings from last night were back, except now Emerson was just a few inches away, there to see it all.

"You know," Emerson said, "parents can be real jerks sometimes, huh?"

I nodded. "My dad, anyway." That was all I could say without the tears threatening to escape.

"Yeah," he said. "Mine too. Both of my parents, actually."

I looked at him, not believing he was opening up to me. To anyone. "I'm sorry."

He shrugged.

We were quiet again, both of us staring down at the green grass.

"My sister's always been there for us, though," he said. "When my parents couldn't or wouldn't, she's there. So at least there's that."

I smiled. "That's my mom. It's always been the two of us because my grandparents passed away before I was born, but she's always been like two parents in one. And a really good friend, actually."

Saying that out loud made me smile but a couple of tears also ran down my cheek. "Sorry," I said, embarrassed that Emerson was watching me cry. I turned to wipe them away.

But before I could do that, he was doing it, his hand carefully touching my cheek.

Slowly, I turned back to him, not knowing what to do besides look at him. My breathing became fast, and my heart raced, even after his hand went back to his side.

His eyes stayed locked on my face for several seconds before meeting my gaze. "I'm kind of glad that I decided to give summer school a real try this year," he said. "Because it meant getting to know you."

I smiled.

"I mean, graduating is nice, too, but…" His voice faded.

His words had me reliving every moment we'd spent together this summer—that first day at the nursing home, dancing with him as we held on to each other, that night at the park.

Did he mean that he felt the same way about me as I did about him? My heart screamed yes.

Then Emerson leaned in, and I asked myself if I was really going to let myself do this.

My heart whispered, *Here's that summer adventure.*

Maybe he'd break my heart for real, but I also needed to do this and not let love slip by.

Emerson took his time, his mouth just centimeters from my own and his nose touching mine. Maybe he was fighting some kind of inner battle too. One I wanted his heart to win.

"Harper?" he whispered.

My phone went off, and I jumped. Emerson sat back.

Our moment was gone, and all I wanted to do was turn my phone to do not disturb.

But it was my mom's face on the screen, and I realized it was lunch time. She had to be checking in. "Sorry, it's my mom," I said, hardly looking up at Emerson.

I took the call. "Hey, mom."

Her voice greeted me right away. "Hey, honey, I

can't talk long, but I just feel horrible about last night."

I looked down. "It's okay, Mom. Really. I think it's for the best. And you know it's not your fault, right?"

She sighed on the other end of the call. "I know. I just…I was thinking. Let's make the best of this. I decided to come in and work some overtime today so we can get away this weekend. Just me and you. Road trip to the beach. How does that sound?" Now she sounded like her usual self. Bright and chipper and happy.

And so did I. "Oh my gosh! Really? Are you sure?"

"I've already booked it, sweetie! We're going to Savannah!"

I shrieked into the phone again, and Emerson chuckled beside me. "I can't wait! When do we leave?"

"Don't unpack your things. We leave early in the morning."

And just like that, things had turned out even better.

We hung up, and I turned to Emerson, trying not to blush from our almost-kiss. "Sorry, that was my mom. She surprised me with our own trip. We haven't taken a vacation in like forever."

Emerson smiled. "Promise you'll bring me back a souvenir?"

SEVENTEEN

W hen I got home, I could hardly sit still. But I had nothing to do because my bags were already packed.

I made my way through the house, washing dishes and wiping down bathrooms, but a couple hours in, I had nothing to do again.

Laying on the couch, I texted my friends a cute selfie and the good news.

Ella: YAY for summer adventure!

Rey: I'm so jealous! The beach beats walking around museums and tourist sites all day :(

Tori: The beach sounds amazing...

Lena: Maybe you'll meet a beach hottie over the weekend ;)

I was sure Lena was just joking, but her comment only made me think of Emerson.

That was twice we had almost kissed. I thought before that it was just me or that whatever we had didn't really mean anything, but the way he looked at me today...

I had to mean something to him, right?

Enough to break his rule of no relationships?

For now, there wasn't much I could do about the situation. My mom and I were leaving in the morning for the beach. Just thinking about not seeing Emerson for two days felt really hard, as excited as I was to get away.

After a few minutes, my eyelids grew heavy. Pulling a heavy blanket over shoulders, I let thoughts of Emerson be the last thing on my mind before sleep took over.

When I woke up an hour later, night was settling in. I got up, closed the curtains, and made sure the front door was locked.

Then I dug out the leftovers from last night. The fridge was full of them.

After I finished eating dinner, I counted down the hours until my mom would be home. Probably around midnight. Because of my nap, I wasn't sleepy at all, so I grabbed my phone and settled onto the couch again, this time with Netflix on.

My phone buzzed with a notification. A familiar name lit up my screen. I had a friend request from Emerson Lopez.

I sat up, a smile on my face.

Maybe he was thinking about me?

Or maybe he wanted to talk about our project due in a week?

No, he had to be thinking about me, right? Maybe he was just as bored as I was tonight.

I accepted his friend request and waited.

Part of me wanted to send him a message right away, ask him what he was up to, but I knew it was probably better to let him make the first move, since he was the one who'd sent the friend request in the first place.

Sure enough, a minute later, my phone buzzed with a new message, and I almost fell off the couch with excitement.

New message from Emerson Lopez.

I opened the message right away, completely forgetting about the movie still playing on the TV. For once, Peter Kavinsky could wait.

Emerson: Hey…

Harper: Hi :)

I bit my lip, not believing I was messaging with Emerson. I turned off the TV and headed upstairs to my room. It was finally starting to get late, and I didn't want to fall asleep on the couch again.

Emerson: What are you up to?

Harper: Nothing much. Kind of bored actually.

Putting my phone on my nightstand, I headed into the bathroom to brush my teeth, too anxious to wait by the phone.

About to wash off my makeup, I snuck over to my phone instead. I shrieked when I found another message from Emerson. I sat on my bed to read it.

Emerson: I thought you'd be out on a Friday night.

Harper: Not with my best friends out of town. Stuck home alone.

I waited for him to say something, but several minutes passed and nothing.

Maybe he'd fallen asleep? It was only nine o'clock, though. Surely, he was at a party or something. I couldn't expect him to keep talking to me.

I lay down, staring up at my phone and feeling lonely all over again.

I settled for browsing social media and then my favorite: Pinterest.

Then a new message.

Emerson: Um, mind opening your window? ;)

WHAT?

I sat straight up and looked around. My room was on the second floor. No way he could just climb in. And I wasn't sure I wanted him to. Just the idea of having a boy in my room made me want to freak out.

Not just because it was my mom's #1 rule, but because I would likely turn into the most awkward human being ever.

Ever.

Emerson: Please? I really don't want to crash into your window :)

I got up and inched my way to my window. Pushing aside my sheer curtains, I looked down to my driveway, and sure enough, there was Emerson. He had on a black leather jacket and a daring grin. My hand came to my mouth, and I couldn't help but laugh.

Wondering where he'd left his skateboard tonight, I noticed a motorcycle stood across the street.

I could have screamed. A motorcycle and a black leather jacket? If Emerson Lopez wasn't the definition of bad boy, I didn't know what was.

He waved to me and took a few steps back. I pushed my window up and peeked out. "I can't believe you."

But he didn't give me the chance to say much else because then he was running toward the tree just a few feet from my window.

He was like Spiderman, jumping from the tree to the siding on the house then a branch and then I jumped back, hands to my mouth again.

Just like that, he came in through my window feet-first, like it was no big deal to jump into a room on the second floor.

He gave me a sheepish grin. "Ever since I saw that on one of those Twilight movies, I always wanted to try that."

I laughed. "Oh my gosh. Well, I'm glad you didn't break your neck because that would have been—"

"Embarrassing," he finished for me. He took a step closer.

I automatically took a tiny step back, still completely surprised how we'd gone from a friend request to this in a matter of minutes. "I have a front door, Emerson!"

He laughed. "So? Where's the fun in that?"

I shook my head at his words but smiled because he was right in front of me. "We should head downstairs."

"Why?" he said. "Your mom's not home."

I crossed my arms. "So? You cannot be in my room."

He came closer, and this time, I didn't back away. "You are a total good girl, aren't you?"

I opened my mouth to say something, anything, but I couldn't, not with the look on his face, the one that made my stomach melt into putty.

"Fine," he said, with a gleam in his eye. "We'll go downstairs."

I led him down to the living room. He stopped at the pictures of me and my mom hanging up on the wall.

"You were a fat baby," he said, chuckling.

Clearly, I did not think this through.

He turned to me. "A cute fat baby, though," he said.

"What are you doing here?" I asked with a small smile. "Do you even have a license to drive that bike out there?"

He shrugged. "Maybe. Maybe not. But you said you were bored. I was bored."

What was that look in his eyes?

"And maybe I wanted to hang out with you," he said. "If you don't mind?"

Thankful I hadn't washed off my makeup after all, I shook my head. "Want to watch a movie?"

We sat down on opposite ends of the couch, and I put on a movie. Definitely not *To All the Boys*. That would have been too awkward. "Do you like *Friends*?" I asked.

"Who doesn't?" he said with a wink.

Before long, though, we were doing more talking than watching. I hugged a pillow to my chest. It still felt like I was breaking the rules, but I reminded myself that I wasn't doing anything wrong. Other than having a boy on my couch without my mom knowing.

I made a mental note to introduce my mom to Emerson after we got back from our trip, and then I was able to relax.

He asked me about my friends, and I told him about them.

"Lena's like this soccer warrior princess," I said. "Total daredevil. But a lot of fun. And Ella is smart with a really good heart. Tori, she kind of tells you how it is. She's honest and strong. Then there's Rey. She is so sweet and creative. She's always doodling and writing."

"You guys sound like a team of girl Power Rangers or something," he said. "Like each of you has these unique powers."

That made me laugh, and then he was laughing. When we finally stopped, he said, "What about you, Harper?"

I looked away. "I don't know."

His voice made me turn toward him. "I think you're kind, like you always see the good in someone. No matter what." He reached over and touched my hand. "You're beautiful, inside and out."

Had I just heard him right? My heart palpitated, and I could hardly find my voice.

Squeezing his hand, I said, "And I think there's more to you than you let on." I locked my eyes on his and said what was on my mind, pretending I was as daring as Lena for just a few seconds. "Underneath that tough exterior, there's this person who brings little old ladies their favorite flowers and—"

But he was already coming in closer.

Headlights filled the living room for a second, and I pulled away instantly.

I jumped up and peeked out the window. "It's my mom!" I said, panicking.

Emerson stood up.

"You've got to go," I said. "She cannot find out you're here!"

I grabbed his hand and led him to the back door, the one in the kitchen. Unlocking it, I practically pushed him outside, my hands on his chest. "Sorry!" I said.

But it wasn't like I was giving him much time to say anything back. He stepped away from the door.

Before I could close the door in his face, I stopped. "Emerson, wait. Before you go…"

Praying my mom didn't walk straight into the kitchen, I tugged on his shirt and pulled him to me. I closed my eyes, leaned my head slightly to the right, and found his mouth. Then my hands went up and around his neck.

And then Emerson kissed me back.

Fireworks could have gone off, and I wouldn't have noticed the difference between them and my hammering heart.

Then I pushed him away, realizing what I had just done. Why had I just done that? At this moment?

Emerson stared back at me, mouth slightly open, his hands on my waist.

"You have to go," I breathed.

But before I could say anything else, he pulled me to him, and he closed the distance between us again. He kissed me like there was just this one and only chance to get it right.

Wishing I could stay in his arms forever, I made myself pull back. The sound of the front door being unlocked reminded me why he had to go. I think it reminded Emerson too because he gave me one last look and disappeared.

Then I quietly closed and locked the back door, leaning my back against it and not believing I had just kissed Emerson Lopez.

EIGHTEEN

E merson and I talked non-stop over the weekend. Even though relaxing on the beach was like nothing else, I still missed him.

What I would have done to relive our kiss from the other night. Or simply see him again.

"Is it just me or are you on your phone more than usual?" My mom asked with a sly smile. "Are you talking to a boy?"

Waves hit the shore, the sound reaching us all the way on the sand. I never wanted to forget the sound.

I smiled, unable to meet her eyes. "Yeah," I confessed.

My mom turned toward me, her sunglasses resting on top of her head. "What's his name?" she asked.

"Emerson," I said.

She thought for a moment. "Where have I heard that name before?"

I shifted so I was facing her, making sure the sun hit my back. There were only a couple hours of sunlight left, and I wanted to take in as much of it as possible while we were here. "He volunteers at the nursing home with me."

"Ah," she said. "Is he cute?"

I nodded. "Totally. He's kind of rough around the edges, but he's so sweet once you get to know him."

"Hmm. Well, I want to meet him," she said. "Make sure you invite him to dinner when we get back."

I smiled wide and texted Emerson right away, letting him know what he was in for.

"Now, tell me more about this boy, Emerson," my mom said.

Girl talk with my mom? This was the best trip ever. I still missed the #BFFs, but even so, this moment felt pretty good.

———

I OPENED the front door to find Emerson waiting there. He came in, a small dish in his hands. "Hey," he said. "My sister made this. I think it's—"

Before he could go on, I put my arms around him and hugged him. Using his free arm, he hugged me back.

"I missed you too," he whispered, leaning his head on mine.

I heard a small cough behind us, and I pulled away and found my mom standing in the doorway to the kitchen. "Mom," I said, a little embarrassed. "This is Emerson."

Emerson stepped forward, and I took the small casserole dish. "Nice to meet you, Mrs. Lee."

She took his hand with a big smile. "And you, Emerson. Harper's told me so much about you."

That comment had Emerson giving me a nervous look, but I took his hand.

Mom's eyes went to the dish in my hand.

I held it up. "Emerson said his sister made this for us."

He nodded. "It's her specialty. She thought it would be a great dessert to have with the chicken parmesan."

My mom gave him an impressed look and winked at me. "Oh…I can't wait to try it."

She took the dish from me, and we followed her into the kitchen. The dining table was already set, and it wasn't long before we were eating together around our small dining table.

I could tell Emerson was nervous. He sat across from me, hardly eating a thing and constantly staring down at his plate.

Just glad he was finally meeting my mom, I glanced at him every few seconds during the dinner conversation. Thankfully, my mom was good at filling in all the awkward pauses.

Emerson answered her questions politely, if not curtly. Wanting him to relax and know that everything was going great, I reached my foot across to his under the table.

When he looked up at me, I smiled, and he finally seemed to exhale and relax.

He actually laughed at something my mom said about the number of skateboard accidents she saw each week. "I've definitely had my share of uh… maneuvers gone wrong. I've landed on my face, on my butt, almost broke my arm once."

I put down my fork. "I don't know how you do it. How do you even attempt something new?"

He shrugged. "You just do it. Flying through the air, sticking a landing…it's the best feeling."

My mom nodded. "I guess it's comparable to a runner's high."

Emerson agreed. "Definitely. Except maybe I'd say it's closer to skydiving or something. Which, I'd actually love to do someday."

I gasped. "I would die of fear. What if I forgot what to do, how to unlock the parachute or whatever?" I contemplated the scenario, closing my eyes, and shook my head. "Nope, nope. I just couldn't."

Emerson laughed. "Or bungee jumping."

Mom stood up, grabbing our empty plates. "I draw the line at bungee jumping," she said. "Voluntarily jumping toward my own death? Do you know the percentage of accidents that happen? No thanks."

With that, she walked off toward the sink, and Emerson and I smiled at each other.

This time, he touched my foot under the table.

"You have to go skydiving with me one day," he said quietly.

"Did you not hear me?" I insisted. "I would die!"

"I meant together," he said. "We'd hold onto each other the whole way down."

That had my heart doing all kinds of funny things, like not beating right.

How did Emerson just say things like that out loud? Did he enjoy making me blush on purpose?

My mom came back with dessert. "Oh, Emerson. This looks amazing. Tell me what it's called again."

"Chocoflan," he said. "Chocolate cake and flan."

I took a bite, and the two textures made my taste buds explode. "This is the most delicious thing I've ever tasted," I said, staring at Emerson.

He popped a second piece into his mouth like it was no big deal that we were eating the most perfect dessert in the world.

"Emerson, you have to tell your sister that this is amazing," my mom said between bites. "All other dessert is now ruined for me."

I nodded. "Agreed. You get to have this all the time?"

He shrugged. "Birthday parties. Holidays. For no good reason. Sure," he joked.

"I have a feeling I'll be saying hello to the five pounds I just lost," my mom said. "You, young man, are officially my favorite. For the sole reason of this chocks-flang."

We laughed at my mom's attempt at pronouncing the name of the dessert.

After dinner, we helped my mom clear the table until she insisted we sit in the living room for a few minutes while she finished up.

She winked at me as we left, and I couldn't believe how well tonight was going.

When we sat on the couch, Emerson pulled me in close.

I smiled up at him. "Keep that up, and she'll want to adopt you," I teased. "Excellent manners and a chocolate dessert? My mom loves you."

Emerson grinned. "Good. You don't know how nervous I was. I've never met a girl's parents before," he said.

That comment had me thinking all kinds of things, mainly what I'd heard about Emerson not doing relationships.

What were we, then? He wouldn't meet my mom if he didn't see us officially together, did he?

I wished he would ask me to be his girlfriend. Then these doubts would disappear. But for someone who usually sensed the right thing to say, I was coming up blank.

I was terrified of ruining tonight, of pushing him away.

What if he just closed back up? Or admitted that this was nothing serious to him?

I bit my lip, trying not to think about it. I just wanted to enjoy tonight. Whatever we had was still entirely new. We could always talk about it some other time.

So instead, I lay my head on his shoulder and took in his smell, listening to him talk about how happy his sister would be that we'd enjoyed her dessert.

When it was time for Emerson to go, I walked him outside. "No motorcycle tonight?" I asked.

He shook his head. "Nah. My brother almost

killed me last time for taking it."

I shook my head but smiled.

Emerson picked up his skateboard.

"Are you sure you don't want a ride home?" I asked. "My mom wouldn't mind."

"It's okay," he said. "I love skateboarding at this time. It's the perfect temperature. And I don't live too far."

He came in close and leaned his head down toward me. Letting my eyes shut on their own, my lips moved against his, and for a few seconds, I forgot about everything except the way he tasted.

Emerson pulled away, but it was like he realized he wasn't done yet because he came in again, and this time, I wrapped my arms around him. He did the same.

We pulled away, my heart going a million miles an hour.

"See you on Monday?" he asked, his hand sweeping hair out of my face.

I nodded, unable to form the words.

He set his skateboard down on the ground, about to get on it.

"Emerson?" I said.

He looked at me.

"No more coming in through my window," I teased.

He bit his lip and smiled.

Then he was gone, and I stood there, completely in awe of the amazing kisser that was Emerson Lopez.

NINETEEN

B ack in my room, I felt like I was floating on air I was so happy.

I opened up the #BFF messages thread right away, knowing they had to be the first ones to hear how tonight had gone.

They'd blown up my phone when I'd told them about Emerson sneaking in my window and then kissing him right before shoving him out the back door.

Now I sent them a message, telling them tonight had been perfect.

A few seconds later, my phone buzzed.

Lena: EMERGENCY VIDEO CHAT

Ella: ^

Tori: I want details!

Rey: !!!

A few minutes later, they all shrieked and screamed and demanded I tell them everything.

Ella smiled from her bed in Puerto Rico. "This is

so exciting! I can't believe you're going out with Emerson."

Tori nodded. "Good for you, Harper."

Lena raised her hands. "I'll be the first to admit it. I was wrong. Maybe there's more to Emerson Lopez than everyone thinks.

"Definitely," I said. "My mom adores him."

"Now tell us everything," Rey said, pen and paper in her hand as usual.

When I was done, Rey sighed dreamily, and everyone else had on puppy love expressions.

"So romantic," Ella said.

Tori stared back at me, a smile on her face. "I can't believe he's your boyfriend. Who would have thought? Then again…good girl Harper and bad boy Emerson…"

Rey spoke up. "It sounds like a movie or something."

Everyone nodded, but I tried to figure out how to say what was on my mind.

"What are you thinking?" Ella asked.

I looked down at my comforter. "It's just that…he hasn't actually asked me to be his girlfriend. How do you know if you are or not? Especially if what he's said is true…that he doesn't do relationships?"

I bit my lip, wondering what my friends had to say about it. For once, no one had anything to say.

Then Tori said, "Maybe he will ask you."

Ella nodded. "Yeah, maybe just give him a little more time."

Rey looked up. "How long is too long, though?"

Ella shrugged. "He did meet your mom. If that doesn't say in a relationship, I don't know what does."

Lena came in toward the screen. "Or just ask him yourself. Ask him if he wants to be your boyfriend."

I scoffed. "I could never do that."

She shrugged. "Why not? I've done it."

Everyone laughed. Typical Lena. Of course, it was no big deal for her. But just kissing Emerson had used up all my courage, and it felt like I was out.

I liked what Ella had said, though. Maybe I just needed to give it a little more time. This was still new.

And what Emerson and I had? It was real.

It had to be.

———

BETWEEN SNEAKING kisses at the nursing home and completing homework during movie time, Emerson and I prepared for our big community fundraiser coming up in a couple of weeks.

"Are you sure this isn't a little, uh, overboard?" he asked, watching me cut out golden stars and add them to the huge pile on the table.

"Are you kidding?" I asked. "This place is going to look magical."

The theme was Dancing with the Stars, except the stars in our case were the senior citizens at the nursing home. Plus I'd be wearing a glamorous dress. I'd already found one for a steal at the local thrift shop.

Everyone would be in their Sunday best, and I couldn't wait.

"How's the playlist coming along?" I asked.

He gave me a thumbs up. "Good. I'm almost done. I already got down all of Ms. Ellie's requests. That alone is about thirty percent of the playlist for the night."

I smiled. "This dollar dance is gonna be so much fun."

He took my hand. "I've already got my dollar ready to go," he said with a wink. "And I'm not talking about dancing with Ms. Ellie."

I laughed. "You know she's gonna make you dance with her. Along with every other lady here."

He fake sighed. "Just the price of being young and handsome, I guess. The ladies can't resist."

We laughed. I pictured him dancing with every little old lady here, and my heart just about burst.

Next, I found Ms. Ellie, and we worked on the flyer announcing the dollar dance fundraiser.

When we finally got it just right, she clapped. "Oh, these contraptions are wonderful," she said, admiring the ancient desktop at the front desk.

I held up a printed copy. "Ms. Moreau said I could hand these out at school tomorrow. Any summer school student who shows up gets extra credit, so I think we could really draw a big crowd."

Her eyes lit up. "Oh, this dance is going to be like reliving my youth. It's been too long since I danced all evening." She left with a wink.

I found Emerson with Mr. Roberts. He didn't look so well today. A thin sheen of sweat covered his forehead, and he looked more tired than usual.

"Is he okay?" I asked Emerson.

Mr. Roberts opened his eyes. "I'm just tired, is all. I think I need to lay down a mo'."

Emerson led him away to a room with a bed in it.

"I'll find Ms. Nancy," I called after him.

A few minutes later, she was at his side, double-checking all his vitals.

Emerson came over, but he could hardly tear his eyes away from Mr. Roberts.

"Is he going to be okay?" I asked, putting my hand on his arm.

He shrugged. "I don't know. He seems off to me."

I squeezed his hand. "Maybe he's just extra tired today. I'm sure he'll be better tomorrow."

He nodded, but even so, it was like he was hardly listening to me.

"Come on," I said. "We should get going, or we'll miss the bus. Maybe we can check in tomorrow at lunch."

"Okay," he said. "You're right."

But the entire walk back to school, Emerson seemed to withdraw back into himself, and all I could do was hold onto his hand and hope all would be better tomorrow.

TWENTY

B ut things weren't better the next day.

In fact, they were worse than we ever could have imagined.

As soon as Emerson and I walked into the nursing home, we knew something was wrong. The entire atmosphere was off. Instead of everyone being lively, they were still and somber. The whole place was too quiet.

Ms. Ellie came right over, a tissue in her hands. I'd never seen her without a smile on her face.

"What's wrong?" I asked her, and her face fell.

"It's Mr. Roberts," she said, her voice breaking. Suddenly, she looked entirely too small and thin and frail.

Emerson headed to the front desk right away, and with one last empathetic look to Ms. Ellie, I followed him there.

What had Ms. Nancy just said to Emerson? Had I heard her correctly?

"A heart attack?" I asked her in disbelief.

She nodded solemnly. "I'm afraid so. It occurred late last night. Mr. Roberts is in the intensive care unit at the hospital right now. We're not sure when he'll be back. I think he was still in critical condition last time I called."

Emerson bit his lip, hardly looking at either of us. Why wasn't he saying anything? What was going through his mind?

I thanked Ms. Nancy, and we walked back to the benches in front of school. Lunch didn't end for another half hour, and I had a feeling Emerson would rather not start our time at the nursing home early today.

In fact, he didn't look like he was up for anything.

"I'm really sorry, Emerson," I said quietly. "I know Mr. Roberts means a lot to you."

The sky was gray, the sun hidden somewhere, and I couldn't help but feel that it was a perfect reflection of Emerson at the moment.

"Ms. Nancy gave me Mr. Roberts's room number," I said, handing him the little piece of paper. "Maybe we can go see him."

He took the paper in his hand, crumpled it up, but didn't say anything.

Slowly, I put my hand on top of his and squeezed, but even so, Emerson wouldn't look at me, wouldn't talk to me.

So I just held his hand and sat there with him. After a while, by the time we were supposed to be at the nursing home, he got up. I stood up with him. "I know maybe you don't want to go to the nursing home today. But maybe we could go study for our math final in the library instead? I bet Ms. Moreau would understand."

Nothing.

"Or, if you're feeling up to it, we could even go visit—"

But he shook his head and grabbed his skateboard. "I have to go."

"Emerson, wait," I started, but he got on his skateboard in a flash and pushed off from the ground.

I tried to go after him, but I knew it was useless.

Emerson was gone.

———

EMERSON DIDN'T SHOW up for school the next day. Or for our afternoon at the nursing home.

He missed both the math and social studies exams the next day. Plus we had the dollar dance community fundraiser coming up. He couldn't give up on everything now, not when he was so close to passing.

Anxious about his grades and mine, I texted him, but he never replied.

Not the first time, or the second time, or the third time.

I wondered if he was okay, and it seemed like I was the only one who cared. The only one who missed him, missed his touch, his smile. His crazy skateboard stunts.

The only other person who asked about him was Ms. Ellie.

She was still upset about Mr. Roberts. He still wasn't out of the woods with the heart attack, and I could tell she had feelings for him.

"My daughter took me to see Mr. Roberts just yesterday," she confessed. "He asked about Emerson, but I didn't know what to tell him. I didn't want to worry him, so I just said he was busy with schoolwork, but that we were all thinking of him."

I exhaled, blinking back tears. "Aw, I miss Mr. Roberts." And I missed Emerson too. "I'm going to go see him today if I can. And I'm going to try to track down Emerson too."

"I don't blame him," she said, wiping at her nose. "It's not an easy thing, realizing your loved ones can be gone, just like that."

Her lip trembled, and I took her hand. I couldn't imagine how hard this was for her. She'd lost her husband, and now another dear friend of hers was in danger of leaving us all too soon.

I left the nursing home and pulled out my phone. I found Emerson's name and pressed the call button. Once again, no answer.

I sent a message instead, pleading with him to come back to school. Surely the teachers would understand and let him make up the exams. But he couldn't give up, not now.

I told him how much I missed him. That I was there for him, that everything would be okay.

Then I stared at my screen, hoping he would say something back. Anything. But a message never came.

Instead of going home, I texted my mom, asking if she could pick me up. Ms. Nancy said Mr. Roberts was finally out of intensive care, which meant he could handle more visitors, at least for a few minutes.

She picked me up, and we went by the store. I knew how depressing hospital rooms could be, so I picked out a few bright balloons, a get well card, and some nice flowers.

Then she drove us to the hospital.

When we got there, she said, "Are you sure you want to do this, honey? I want to warn you. Mr. Roberts might not look like his usual self."

I nodded and thought about what she meant. But I had to do this. It was the least I could do. "Let's go."

Mr. Roberts was on the fourth floor, on the cardiac wing. My mom led us straight there.

We stopped in front of his room, and she looked at me. "Want me to go in there with you? Or I can wait out here?" she asked.

I smiled. "It's okay. I won't be long."

She nodded. "I'll be right over there."

Slowly opening the door, I walked in.

Mr. Roberts wasn't alone.

A familiar face turned toward me.

"Emerson," I said, the balloons I carried still in my hands.

He looked away.

Mr. Roberts was asleep, a thin white blanket up to his chest. A couple of balloons already hung around his room, and I added mine to the mix. Then I carefully walked around his bed and placed the flowers on the nightstand near his bed.

I turned to Emerson. "Have you been here long?" I asked.

He shrugged. "Not too long, I guess."

I walked over and sat down next to him. His chair was pulled up right next to Mr. Roberts. "It's good that you came."

He sighed, and I could see how hard this was for him.

I wanted to reach for his hand, but I wasn't sure if that was what Emerson wanted. He felt different, sad and still closed off. Like he didn't want to give away how he was really feeling.

A plate of cookies sat on the nightstand next to Emerson. I recognized the container with the red lid, like the one his sister had packed the dessert in when Emerson had come over for dinner.

"Did you bring him those?" I asked quietly.

He glanced at the cookies and then at me before going back to staring at Mr. Roberts. "Oatmeal raisin. They're his favorite."

"That's really sweet of you," I said. "Ms. Ellie said he was asking about you the other day. He's going to be really glad that you came."

Emerson bit his lip and cleared his throat. Tears welled up in my eyes just watching how hard he was holding his own back.

Emerson sniffed. "I heard the doctor say his chances aren't good," he whispered. "His heart…"

I took his hand, and he held on tight. "All we can do is be here for him and hope he gets better. Mr. Roberts…he's a fighter," I said.

Emerson nodded, and then he slipped his hand out of mine.

"He's going to be okay," I said, seeing how distraught he looked.

He shook his head. "You don't know that. No one knows if he's going to be okay, if he's going to be able to go back—"

He stood up, and I did the same. Grabbing his jacket, he moved to the door.

"Emerson, wait," I began. "You can't just keep disappearing."

He paused for a second. "This was all a big mistake."

Then he opened the door and left. I went after him, not wanting him to just leave again and not hear from him for days.

A mistake? What did he mean? Summer school? Trying so hard? Us?

All of it?

I shut the door silently behind me and searched for him. He was already halfway down the hall.

Speeding after him, I dodged nurses and people with carts. It was going to be impossible to catch up to him at this rate.

Already, the tears were back. I just wanted him to not run away this time.

A hand grabbed my arm, and I spun around.

It was my mom. "Let him go, sweetie."

My face fell, and she pulled me in toward her. I wrapped my arms around her.

"It's okay," she said into my hair. "Some people just need time alone to process things. But don't worry. He'll come around."

Emerson's final words to me still rang in my head. Would he?

TWENTY-ONE

That weekend, my mom came home, and I could tell right away from the tired and sad expression on her face that something was wrong.

I dropped the magazine I'd been reading, my hands covering my mouth.

"I'm so sorry, Harper," she said, sitting down beside me. "He didn't make it." She put her arms around me. "Mr. Roberts passed away early this morning."

I sobbed into her shoulder, wondering how Emerson, Ms. Ellie, and everyone else had to be taking the bad news.

"His family was with him the whole time," she said. "He didn't feel a thing. It happened in his sleep."

I nodded. It was the best we could have asked for, given the circumstances. Mr. Roberts had survived a war, had a family, and lived a long life.

But somehow, it still didn't feel fair.

My mom kissed my head after a few minutes. "I'm going to make us something to eat. Warm chicken noodle soup will help. I promise. And I was thinking maybe we could take some to the nursing home today?"

I put my arm around her. "That would be great, Mom. Thank you. Maybe I can make some cookies. Emerson said oatmeal raisin was Mr. Roberts's favorite."

She smiled, resting her hand on my cheek. "I'm so proud of you, Harper. Never forget that."

We got to work cooking and baking, and my mind went to Emerson. I could hardly focus on the directions for the cookies.

I wondered if he even knew.

Telling my mom I was going to the bathroom, I headed to the living room and grabbed my phone.

There was a new email from Ms. Moreau to both of us, letting us know what had happened.

So he probably did know.

Even so, I typed out a new message to him, letting him know what had happened and that I'd be there for him no matter what. That Mr. Roberts would want us to celebrate his life, not be sad over the fact that he was gone.

I remembered the pictures we took the afternoon we had all danced together at the nursing home not too long ago. The one of Ms. Ellie and Mr. Roberts had me tearing up again, but I selected it and sent it to Emerson.

My messages to him immediately changed from

delivered to read. Which was more than he had done the past several days.

Three dots showed up, and I waited for him to say something, but then they went away.

Nothing.

I sent him a simple heart emoji and put my phone away.

I couldn't imagine what he was going through right now. After spending all summer with sweet Mr. Roberts, Emerson had to be devastated. I tried to imagine losing Ms. Ellie, and it just made me cry again.

Poor Ms. Ellie. I remembered the dance she'd had with Mr. Roberts, the bright smiles on both their faces that day.

As sad as I was, I was also really grateful to have known Mr. Roberts and to have ended up in the nursing home this summer.

Ms. Ellie had quickly become special to me, and I could tell Mr. Roberts had been like that for Emerson.

My heart grieved for the death of the kind old vet and Emerson's loss.

I just hoped Emerson would come back to school, to the nursing home, and to me.

———

TWO DAYS before the dollar dance, the nursing home was almost back to normal. As sad as everyone still was, we were excited for the event coming up.

The ladies had their outfits picked out, and I'd already promised to do everyone's makeup.

Ms. Ellie and I had everything just about ready.

We were only missing our DJ and partner in crime: Emerson.

He still wasn't back. Not at the nursing home or school.

His grades had to be plummeting, but no matter how many times I tried to call or text him, he wouldn't reply. The few times I'd gone to the park looking for him, he hadn't been there, and I hoped he was okay.

One day during lunch I headed to Ms. Moreau's office to see if she had any news.

"I'm afraid this isn't a first for him," she said. "I'm having trouble tracking him down too."

I bit my lip, wishing there was something we could do for him.

Like she was reading my mind, Ms. Moreau said, "All we can do is be there for him. Support him as much as possible. And keep trying to get him to come back to school."

I wondered what good that would be, though. Summer school ended in a few more days, and he'd already missed the last week.

Would our teachers let him make up all the work he'd missed? Would there even be enough time for him to do that?

I tried to remember where he said he lived, and I took the bus there after school.

When I got off the bus, I pulled out my phone,

texting my mom that I'd be downtown grabbing a bite to eat and doing some window shopping. I walked until I found the street he'd mentioned. My phone said I was in the right spot, but I had no idea which house was his.

I made my way down the street, sweat dripping down my forehead and neck from the hot afternoon sun, wondering if I'd run into him or one of his brothers. I remembered what one of them looked like from last semester, but I didn't see any of them around.

After a while, it was clear that I had no clue what I was doing or where I was going. And I probably looked like a sweaty mess.

My eyes landed on a house with blue shutters and old paint. There was a single car in the driveway, but what stood out to me was the young woman in the garden out front.

Were those daisies? The woman had the same dark hair as Emerson and his brothers, and I wondered if this could be their older sister? A little boy ran up to her, and she turned to hug him.

Running up to the house, I called out, "Hi!"

Taking her little boy's hand in hers, she got up and faced me. She seemed to relax once she saw me.

"Sorry," I said with a smile. "I didn't mean to scare you. I was just wondering…Is this Emerson's house? Are you his sister?"

She blinked a couple times before responding. "Yeah, I'm Yasmin. Who are you?"

Her little boy bent down to play in the dirt at her feet.

I came a little closer. "I'm Harper, a friend of Emerson's from school? We've been worried about him. We haven't seen him in a few days, and he's missing a lot class. If he doesn't come back, he won't earn his credits and be able to graduate on time."

Yasmin nodded. "I've been getting phone calls every day from that counselor. I'll tell you the same thing I told her. Emerson is having a tough time right now. I've tried talking to him, but he won't listen. He's gone all day. I've hardly seen him myself. I have an eighteen-month-old to take care of and a job. I wish I had the time to track him down, but he's almost eighteen. I can't make him go back to school, you know?"

I bit my lip. She was right. "I just wish there was something I could do…"

There was silence, and I wondered if I should just go home and give up on Emerson altogether.

But then Yasmin said something else. "You're the girl he's been seeing, right?"

I looked up at her. "Yeah, I guess so."

"You're the first girl he's ever talked about, Harper. It's hard to tell with Emerson, but I can tell you mean a lot to him."

I gave her a small smile. "Thanks. Your dessert that you made, by the way. It was really good. My mom is still raving about it."

"Thanks," she said, lighting up. "Glad to know someone appreciates my cooking."

There was more silence, and I got ready to say goodbye.

But once again, she beat me to it. "I'm guessing he hasn't told you, but Emerson was really close to our grandpa when he was little. All of us were, before he passed away. I'm guessing that's why all of this has been especially hard on him, you know? Brings back all those memories."

I nodded. "I'm so sorry. I had no idea."

Everything made so much more sense now.

I hadn't been old enough to know my grandparents before they died, but he had. With what I'd heard about the absence of his parents, his grandparents must have been like the parents he'd never had.

My mom was the only real family I had. I didn't know what I'd do if I ever lost her.

My stomach sank. I couldn't imagine the pain Emerson was going through right now.

TWENTY-TWO

I took the bus back to town, my head resting on the window the entire time.

The rumble of the bus down the road felt like the swirl of emotions going on inside me.

Would I see Emerson again? Surely, I'd see him when school started in the fall, but what about the rest of summer? What about us? It felt like we were over, even though it had just begun.

I supposed that answered my question about Emerson and I being in a relationship.

I had crushed on him ever since the first time I'd seen him in the cafeteria when I'd moved here. It had been months of just seeing him from afar and wondering what his voice sounded like, admiring his hair and his confidence, and wondering what went on behind those dark eyes.

Then this summer he'd finally talked to me. We'd become friends. Laughed together. Spent time together.

And become something more.

Only for it all to be gone in an instant.

No closure.

Was it really over? I had to know.

I had to know if he was okay, if there was any way I could be there for him.

The bus came to a stop in front of the park, and I remembered that night with him. Learning how to skateboard and holding on to him so I wouldn't fall.

He'd assured me that he'd never let that happen, that he'd hold on to me.

I wanted to tell him that he had let me fall. Hard. And he wasn't even there to help me back up.

Staring out the window, I noticed a lone figure sitting behind a tree. I could see his long legs.

And a familiar skateboard at his side.

The bus rumbled to life again, and I jumped up.

Running toward the front of the bus, I shouted, "Wait!"

The handful of people on the bus looked up at me. The bus driver looked annoyed, but he pressed on the brakes.

Almost tumbling to the ground, I somehow made it to the double doors and stepped off, shouting a quick thanks behind me. Then I looked toward that tree.

He was still there, a couple hundred feet away. It almost didn't feel real, Emerson so close after not seeing him for so long.

Would he run off as soon as he saw me? Would he even talk to me?

Only one way to find out.

I carefully made my way to that tree. When I was just a few feet away, in the shade of the tree, Emerson turned his head slightly toward me.

I opened my mouth, wondering what was the right thing to say. "Hey," I said.

Nothing. Emerson only looked down, and his fingers tugged at the grass beside him.

"I missed you," I said, creeping a little closer. I kept going until I was beside him.

I kneeled down and sat on the grass, feeling like I was walking on eggshells. Like when I was little, and I'd come upon a deer in the backyard, and I just wanted to get closer without it running away. I never could get close enough.

I could have asked him if he was okay, but I knew he wasn't.

Once again, I felt like I didn't know the right thing to say.

His hand was right there, just inches away, and I wanted to take it so bad.

But I knew there was a good chance he'd pull it away, and I didn't want to touch him if that wasn't what he wanted.

His voice startled me. "What are you doing here?" He still wouldn't look at me.

"I've been looking everywhere for you," I said softly. "I've been worried. I saw you, and I just wanted to see how you were."

He exhaled. "Well, you've seen me. You can go. I can't do this right now."

"You don't have to do anything," I said. "I just wanted to tell you that I'm here for you, no matter what, Emerson. I'm here. I know—"

He sat up, his back no longer resting on the tree. He finally looked at me, and those dark eyes were full of anger and hurt and something else. "I just want to be alone. Why doesn't everybody get that? I'm not interested in school or grades or any of it. I'm not going back. Not now and not in the fall. So just go."

His words, the anger in them, stung, and I bit my lip to keep from crying.

Nodding my head, I said, "Okay. Maybe with a little more time—"

"I don't need any more time to think about it, Harper. I just—" His voice cracked, and pain flashed across his face. His hands came up to his temples and his legs to his chest.

I scooted closer. Holding my breath, I slowly put my hand on his shoulder. He felt tense under my touch, but after a second, he relaxed. "It's okay," I whispered. "It's okay to feel like this."

Only the sound of our breathing reached my ears for the next several seconds. That and the sound of traffic and honking in the distance.

Maybe he was letting me back in.

Please, just let me back in, I wanted to say.

Emerson looked up slowly, letting his hands go to his lap. He turned to me and met my gaze, all the pain still there. He reached his hand over and caressed my cheek, his eyes going to my mouth.

For the first time in what seemed like forever, we were close again, and it felt like coming home.

He got even closer, his face right in front of mine and his hand still on my cheek.

"Harper," he said, his voice low.

Then his lips pressed against mine, moved against mine.

My whole body relaxed, and I held on to him, terrified of stumbling again.

I didn't know long we kissed like that, but it ended way too soon.

Emerson pulled back, both of us breathless.

The sun was no longer visible in the summer sky, and in the back of my mind, there was this tiny unimportant worry of letting my mom know where I was.

I tried to read Emerson, but he pulled all the way back, his hands on his knees again.

Opening my mouth to ask him if he was okay, I stopped when he spoke first.

"I can't do this, Harper," he said.

"What do you mean?" I croaked.

He glanced at me before looking down again. "I'm sorry if I've led you on. That's my fault, and I take full responsibility for it. But I told you. I can't do this."

My mouth fell, and my heart felt like it'd just been run over by an eighteen-wheeler. "What?" I asked.

"I don't do relationships," he said, his voice hard now.

"But—" I started.

"But I can't," he finished for me. "I'm better off alone, and…" His voice died away.

"And what?" I said, fighting the lump in my throat. "And not taking the risk of falling in love?"

His lips pressed into a thin line. "I'm just not interested in doing this."

He stood up, and I did the same.

"Don't do this," I said, tears cascading down my cheeks.

He shrugged. "It's done."

"Let's just talk about this," I said, closing my eyes and trying to understand how this was even happening.

He turned to me. "There's nothing to talk about. This is done. It's over—"

"You can't tell me all of this has meant nothing to you, Emerson," I cried.

He looked away, shoving his hands in his pockets.

I wiped away the tears and tried to calm down. "You can't do this. You can't just cut everyone off because you can't deal with what happened."

He stared at me, anger clear on his face.

"What happened with Mr. Roberts is so sad, Emerson. I can't imagine how hard it must be for you, especially after losing your own grandparents."

His chest rose up and down, his gaze on me.

"But Mr. Roberts—and your grandparents— surely they wouldn't want you to be like this forever. They would want you to move on and be happy and live your life to your fullest potential. Not close your-self off. That's not what life is about."

He didn't say anything, just stared at the ground.

"You have to give life and love a chance, no matter what the risk," I said. "Give us a chance. Please."

"I can't," he uttered. "It's not worth it."

He kicked at the ground, not saying anything else.

Meanwhile, my world shattered all around me.

I tried to step closer to him, but he moved back.

"Emerson," I said. The tears were back.

He looked at me, his eyes sad but determined. "You deserve better than me."

I shook my head, but he was relentless.

"I'm sorry," he said.

Then he walked around me, picked up his skateboard, and disappeared into the night, taking my heart with him.

TWENTY-THREE

I was thankful for the dark empty house that night when I finally got home.

Somehow, I caught the bus home, the last route of the night, trudged up the stairs, and ended up in my bed, under the covers.

After a while, my pillow soaked with tears, I realized I still had my shoes on.

I pulled the sheets tight around me, holding on to whatever I had left.

At some point, I must have fallen asleep, because the rain pattering on my window woke me up the next morning.

I grabbed my phone from my nightstand—dead —and plugged it in. Still numb inside, I walked into the hall bathroom and found my reflection in the mirror.

My blonde hair was a mess, part of it pressed down on one side and the rest looking like it'd gotten into a scuffle with a cat or something.

Plus, I hadn't bothered to wash my makeup off last night, and now I looked like a raccoon in mourning.

Climbing into the shower, I let the warm water attempt to wash away everything that had happened last night.

Emerson's last words to me rang in my head over and over again, and I shut my eyes, the tears re-surfacing. *It's not worth it.*

I made it back to bed, pajamas on, and grabbed my phone.

There were several messages from my friends, from last night and this morning.

Rey: We haven't heard from you in a while, Harp. Everything okay?

That was the last message from my friends.

I sighed, not even knowing where to start.

Harper: Emerson broke up with me…

Right away, little text bubbles showed up on my screen.

Ella: I AM SO SORRY.

Tori: What happened? :(So sorry.

Rey: :(((sorry, friend

Lena: UGHHH. Not cool.

I told them everything, but really, I just wished they were home with me so I wouldn't be alone.

Harper: Tell me you guys are almost home…

Tori: Definitely. Cheer camp ends tomorrow.

Rey: Girls night as soon as we're home! If we can ever finish driving through Texas, then I'll be back before you know it!

Lena: What she said ^ I should be home soon too.

Ella: Count on it. Wish we were there now. My flight leaves tonight. I'll be there before you know it.

Tori: Hang in there, Harp. <3

Harper: Guys, my heart is completely broken :(I guess that's what happens when you fall for the bad boy.

Ella: :(maybe he'll come around.

Lena: He better… I still don't get it.

Tori: Yeah, maybe give it some time. But even if it doesn't work out, everything will be okay <3

Rey: <3 <3 <3

Rey: I think that if it's meant to be, it'll work itself out. And if it's not to meant to be, then there's someone else out there for you, girl.

Harper: I miss you guys <3 :(

They got back to what they were doing, and I went back to moping in bed. But it wasn't long before my mom knocked at my bedroom door.

"Yeah?" I called.

She popped her head in. "Can I come in?"

I nodded, hugging my pillow.

She sat down beside me. "I was wondering why you hadn't come down for breakfast yet. You're usually an early riser no matter how late you go to bed."

I bit my lip, tears welling in my eyes just from her hand on my hair.

"Is this about Emerson?" she asked quietly. "Did you finally get to talk to him?"

All I could do was nod, and then the tears started

up again. Sobs wracked my chest, and I buried my head into my pillow.

"Oh, honey, I'm sorry," she said, hugging me as best she could. She sighed. "Your very first heartbreak is the worst. I remember mine well."

That only made me think of Dad and Mom around my age. Dad breaking her heart for the first time and again and again over the years until she finally walked away, but not before she was pregnant with me.

It almost felt like the past had repeated itself, and then I cried because I should have known better. Should have learned from what my mom and I had already gone through as a result of a bad boy breaking her heart so many years ago.

But it wasn't that easy.

Did we really have a say in who we fell in love with? Or did it just happen?

My head hurt trying to make sense of it all.

I just knew that I should have been angry at Emerson for breaking my heart. But even so, I missed him more than ever.

———

MOM CONSOLED me through the next twenty-four hours. After the boyfriends she'd had throughout the years, she was a pro at it.

There was ice cream, caramel popcorn, specialty dark chocolate, iced coffee, and all the Netflix we could stand.

With her around to pull me back up, the pain of losing Emerson was almost bearable.

At least until she had to go into work the next evening.

Before she left, she kissed me on the forehead. She wore her favorite purple scrubs with the unicorns on them. They were a hit with the kids she took care of the in ER. "I promise I'll be back as soon as I can. Don't wait up, though, because it'll be late. But tomorrow morning. You, me, and a giant plate of French toast, okay?"

I nodded and worked up a feeble smile. "Drive safe," I said.

Then I settled into the couch again, lonely within minutes. I focused on breathing, in and out. The TV was on, but I could hardly focus on it.

How could I watch someone else end up with their Prince Charming or tall, dark, and handsome when I hadn't? It just reminded me of what I didn't have.

My heart still beat inside my chest, but I felt like it had gone missing ever since that night.

Sniffling, I reached for another tissue and let the tears fall once again.

The doorbell rang, and I wondered if it was my mom. Maybe she'd forgotten her phone. She'd only left about fifteen minutes ago.

I got up and made my way to the door, stepping up to the peephole. It definitely wasn't my mom, but already I felt ten times better.

I flung open the door with my first genuine smile in a while.

Before me stood Ella, Tori, Lena, and Rey. They immediately enveloped me in a hug, and I didn't know if I should cry or laugh, so I did both while jumping up and down. "You're here!" I said. "I can't believe it."

They squeezed me back, and I closed my eyes.

Finally, they pulled away, and we stepped inside. I closed the front door behind me. "When did you guys get in?"

Ella took my hand. "We all got here like twenty minutes to an hour ago, but we wanted to come over together."

I took each of them in. They looked so different even though it had only been six weeks. "You guys are so tan," I said. I turned to Lena. "I didn't even think it was possible for you to be more bronzed and toned than you already were."

She struck a pose and gave us a smile worthy of the front cover of Elle. "What can I say?"

We all burst out laughing.

Lena eyed my bare shoulders. "Hey, you're looking pretty sun-kissed yourself."

"Thanks," I said, leading them to the couch. "It's so good to see you guys. You don't even know." I wiped at my eyes.

Tori gave me another hug. "I brought you something," she said. She pulled something from her bag and held it up. It was a bracelet, and it looked hand-made with bright pink and navy blue threads interwoven together. "I made it. This one's for you, and I have the rest. One for each of us."

She put mine on, a huge smile on all of our faces, and then handed the rest out. They were all different colors and each had a different little metal charm.

Mine was a heart. Ella's was a little pair of glasses. Rey's was a book, Tori's was a megaphone, and Lena's was a tiny soccer ball. Of course.

Lena shrieked. "These are awesome!"

The waterworks started up for me again, and they hugged me close.

Rey held up a bag. "I brought you guys something too!"

Apparently, all of them had, and we spent a good hour just going through everything and screaming like hyenas over how cool the souvenirs were.

Rey had brought us t-shirts with funny things on them. Ella brought us candy from Puerto Rico, and Lena had brought us each a really pretty and brightly painted ceramic cowgirl boot from Mexico.

I stared at the bracelet on my wrist, and the array of items in my lap. "It's like Christmas came early. I feel so bad, though. I don't have anything for you guys," I said, tears welling up in my eyes. "And why can't I stop crying?"

I laughed out loud, still super glad that they were back. "Wait," I said, jumping up from the couch. "I do have something."

I ran to my room, found what I was looking for, and ran right back to the living room. Sitting down in front the coffee table, I poured out the gemstones inside the tiny cloth bag. "From my trip to the beach. I know it's not much, but you guys can each have one."

"Ooh," Lena said, kneeling down beside me. "These are pretty."

Ella picked up a clear one. "I like this one."

Lena grabbed a bright orange one. "Can I take this one?" she asked with a smile. She turned it in her hands.

"Of course," I said. I turned to Tori and Rey.

Tori went for the red jasper stone while Rey picked out a teal gemstone. "What's this one called?" she asked.

I shrugged. "I have no idea," I replied. "I just picked out the ones I liked, but I only know the names of a couple of them. " The rose quartz was my favorite, but I picked up a gray metallic looking stone instead. This one felt right for Emerson.

I put the remaining stones back in the little bag, hoping I'd be able to give him his gemstone too.

Rey rested her head on my shoulder. "Thank you," she said. "I love it."

I hugged her.

Rey carefully placed the stone in a small pocket of her jeans. "We've got to hang out these last couple of weeks of summer as much as possible."

Tori smiled. "Done," she said.

"Definitely," Lena said. She held an extra cowboy boot in her hand. It was blue and green and black.

"Who's that one for?" I asked out of curiosity.

She looked down at it. "Ian. Boys' soccer team?

He made me promise him that I'd bring him back something."

Ella and Tori eyed each other, and I wondered if they were thinking the same thing. "Is he one of the boys you've kissed for funsies?" I asked with a wink. Rey sat up.

Lena scoffed. "No way. He's just a friend. Definitely not someone I'd kiss for funsies. Besides, he has a girlfriend now, who's like…" She pretended to stick a finger down her throat. "But anyway!"

Ella lay back on the couch. "What should we do? Movie? Pizza?"

I nodded, hungry all of a sudden. "I could totally go for some pizza."

Ella pulled out her phone. "Just tell me what toppings you guys want."

Lena's eyes lit up. "Oooh, I forgot to tell you guys. My coach says I have a good chance of getting a college scholarship this year. Man, I'd love to play soccer in college."

Then Rey told us about the secret project she was working on. She couldn't give us details yet, but she had big hopes for it and finally sharing some of her writing online.

Meanwhile, I rested my head on Ella's shoulder as we sat on the couch, happy that my friends were back from their summer adventures to spend the last couple weeks before school together.

Summer hadn't gone as planned for me, but I'd be okay. Friends like Ella, Tori, Lena, and Rey were all I needed.

TWENTY-FOUR

E merson was gone from school, the nursing home, and my life, but the show had to go on.

Organizing the dollar dance fundraiser kept me busy during the day, and in the evening, the #BFFs and I made up for lost time.

We went to the pool, to the mall, and hung out at each other's houses.

Little by little, I felt like my heart was recovering, even if I still missed Emerson. I just wanted to get over him, but it was taking time.

The day of the dollar dance, I made sure I had everything I needed in my overnight bag. My outfit, accessories, curling iron, and makeup.

The #BFFs would be there later, but for now, I had to get ready, help decorate the place, and get the music going.

I wasn't very techie, though, so I had a hard time hooking up my phone to the computer and speakers and getting the music to play. After a half hour, I still couldn't get it to work, and I sighed in frustration.

Emerson would have figured this out in two minutes, but I couldn't ask him for help. I knew it was time to call for backup.

Harper: Ella, SOS. I can't figure out how to set the music up!

I sent her a picture, and she replied that she'd be there as soon as she could.

Stepping away from the computer, I glanced around at the nursing home.

We had cleared most of the main room and pushed the chairs toward the walls. The craft room was ready to go with snacks and beverages, and the senior citizens looked adorable in their best outfits, including Ms. Ellie.

All I had left to do was their makeup and then I could get ready myself.

Ms. Ellie had done her hair today, and she looked fabulous with the curls in her blonde hair. After I was done, looked like a fifties movie star with her winged eyeliner and dark red lipstick.

She gave me a huge smile. "Will you look at that? I could pass for Marilyn Monroe herself," she said, patting her hair delicately.

I laughed. "You sure could."

By the time I finished doing all the ladies' makeup, the dollar dance was due to start in a matter of minutes.

I ran to the bathroom with my overnight bag in hand and changed as fast as I could. To keep with the

Dancing with the Stars theme, I'd brought a glittery gold dress that came just above my knees and hugged my curves. I paired it with some strappy high-heeled shoes I'd borrowed from my mom. Then I touched up my makeup and hair, making sure the soft waves in my hair were perfect.

I definitely couldn't do all the fancy moves the dancers on the show could, but thankfully I only had to keep up with seventy-year-olds. And whoever else showed up to pay a dollar to dance with me.

Heading back to the dance, I arrived there just in time to see my friends walk in. They saw me, waved, and came right over.

"You made it!" I said. They were in everything from sundresses and cowboy boots to heels and figure-hugging dresses. "You guys look great."

"Us?" Lena said. "Look at you! You're a doll, Harp!"

She spun me around, and I laughed. "Thanks."

Tori winked. "The boys from school are totally gonna be lining up with cash in hand for a chance to dance with you."

I shrugged. "Well, the school announced the fundraiser tonight, but I'm not sure that many people from school will be coming. They probably have more exciting things to do on a Friday night."

Tori held up her phone. "I don't think so. As far as I know, most of the cheerleaders and jocks will be here."

Lena held up her phone too with a smile. "The soccer team too."

Ella smiled. "We all texted everyone we knew."

Rey nodded. "I hope you bought enough safety pins! But just in case…" She held up a little clear container full of them. Then she patted a small black bag at her side. "I brought my camera too."

They were right. The first hour of the dollar dance was calm and quiet and mostly senior citizens dancing with each other, their families, or my friends, hardly moving from side to side. It was the cutest thing, and we couldn't take enough pictures.

Mrs. Porter nodded in approval. "Those are going to be perfect for the website," she said. "This was a great idea, Harper."

Even Ms. Nancy was getting her groove on in one corner of the dance floor.

By six o'clock, though, the nursing home began to fill up with arrivals. Tons of people from school showed up.

And they were happy to donate a dollar or two for a dance with elderly neighbors or relatives.

Ella kept the music going all night, and she kept it interesting, even if I wondered what Emerson had originally put together.

After Lena led a crazy group dance where I could hardly keep up, I joined Ella for a few quiet moments, just taking it all in. Ms. Ellie hadn't stopped dancing yet, and I was glad she was doing better since Mr. Roberts had passed away.

This dollar dance had turned out way better than I could have hoped for. But even so, something felt off.

Emerson should have been here tonight, and I was sad he was missing it.

This would be over in a couple hours, and then we'd be taking down decorations and counting money.

A group of guys from school made their way to the entrance, getting ready to leave.

Someone came in, holding the door open for them before turning in my direction. He had a small bouquet of flowers in his hand. Daisies. And a skateboard under his other arm.

His eyes met mine, and I froze.

Emerson.

He walked right over. I was speechless.

Finally, I opened my mouth and made the words come out. "What are you doing here?"

Ella played the next song and mouthed *bathroom* before heading off in that direction.

Emerson watched her leave then turned to me. He shrugged. "I just had to see you." He glanced around. "See this before it was over."

There was a hint of sadness in his eyes, and I remembered that the last time he'd been here was when we'd found out about Mr. Roberts' heart attack.

He held up the flowers. "These are for you."

I took them, not sure what to say. "I don't understand," I said. "Why—"

"I just wanted to say I'm sorry," he said. "I wasn't going to come tonight, but I know I promised I'd bring a sound system for the dance. Then Ms.

Moreau came to my house today. She dropped this off."

He set his skateboard down and pulled a folded-up piece of notebook paper out of his pocket. "It's from Mr. Roberts. He had a few things he wanted to say to me, in case…" He exhaled, carefully opening the letter. "He wrote it the night he had his heart attack. Anyway, he reminded me how important you are to me."

Emerson's eyes found mine, and my breath hitched.

Then he stared down at the letter. "How important it is for me to finish school." He shrugged. "So here I am, hoping you'll forgive me for being a jerk to you. Hoping you'll take me back. Maybe keep pushing me like you were in school."

When I didn't say anything, he looked down at me.

Was I hearing him correctly?

My hands came to my mouth for a second. Holding back tears, I took in Emerson, a part of me wondering if I should hand over my heart to him again.

I tried to read what lay behind those dark eyes of his. Maybe I wouldn't always know, but right now, I had a pretty good guess.

Then I closed the gap between us, wrapping my arms around his neck.

I breathed in his scent, shutting my eyes so I could focus on the feel of him, on this moment. "What took you so long?" I said into his jacket.

He chuckled, hugging me back and nuzzling his head in my shoulder, my neck. "I missed you so much."

We pulled back, smiling at each other. I wanted to kiss him to so bad, but he walked over to the computer. He handed Ella a USB, told her something, and she nodded.

Then he glanced toward the door. He waved two guys toward us. I recognized his brothers, each carrying huge speakers and all kinds of fancy-looking equipment.

They got busy setting it all up, and in the meantime, a slow and romantic song came on. Ella winked at us, and Ms. Ellie's voice called to us from the middle of the room.

She held onto one of her grown sons, and they looked adorable. She motioned for us to join them.

Emerson grabbed my hand, I put my flowers down, and he led me to where everyone else was dancing. My friends practically jumped up and down once they saw us together, and my smile couldn't grow any bigger.

He turned around to face me, and we stood for a second.

I took him in. "I'm afraid a dance with me will cost you a dollar," I teased.

He pulled several crumpled dollar bills out of his pocket. "Don't worry. I came prepared."

Rey rushed over with a handful of safety pins, and I laughed out loud. Then she went back to watch us from the sidelines with the rest of the #BFFs, linking her arm with them again.

Meanwhile, Emerson carefully pinned every single dollar bill plus a five-dollar bill he had to me.

"That is a very generous donation," I said when he was done.

Emerson gave me a soft smile. "I'm hoping that covers the rest of the night."

"I'm sure Ms. Ellie will insist on a dance with you, too. before the night is over." I put my arms around him again, and his hands settled on my waist.

"As long as the last dance is with you," he said into my ear.

Shivers ran down my spine, and I closed my eyes, taking in his smell, focusing on his touch, on the feel of his shoulders under my fingers.

We swayed together, and I wanted to lose myself in the relaxing music, but then the song was over.

The next one came on, and it was in Spanish. Now that Emerson's brothers had finished setting up, the music was much louder. Ms. Ellie immediately began some kind of salsa dance move, and I stared back at Emerson. "I can't dance to this kind of music," I confessed, ready to take my place back at the sidelines.

But he took my hand before I could run away. "I'll teach you."

I bit my lip. "I'll just make a fool of myself."

Ms. Ellie danced right over to us. "Harper, just feel the music and let your body move!" She drew out that last word and let it course through the rest of her body. She looked toward Emerson. "By the way, we're very glad to see you're back, Emerson." Then she winked at him and shimmied her way back to her current dance partner.

I giggled. "How does she have so much energy?"

Emerson turned back to me. "I think Ms. Ellie has more energy in her left pinky toe than I do in my whole body."

We went back to the task at hand, and Emerson taught me the steps.

At 8:30, when the dollar dance came to an end, we were the last ones to stop dancing, even after the music ended and the lights came back on.

I didn't want the night to end.

But it was okay, because this dance wouldn't be our last.

EPILOGUE

After a crazy week of finals, summer school came to an end.

My friends took Emerson and me out for ice cream to celebrate.

Ella gave me a hug. "You did it."

I looked to Emerson. "We both did it," I said, squeezing his hand.

Emerson glanced down, but a grin played on his face.

"Congratulations," Tori said, her arm around Noah.

"To both of you," Rey finished.

Lena pointed her thumb at them. "What they said."

Jesse joined us, an ice cream sundae in his hands. "Now you get to do it all over again in a few days when the school year starts."

Lena groaned. "Don't remind me." And we all laughed.

We found a big table with an umbrella and sat down with our ice cream. Ella and Jesse shared their sundae. It was the cutest thing. Then Noah pushed Tori's cone into her face, and we all burst out laughing. I handed her a napkin, and she chased after Noah.

Rey and Lena watched from their seats, egging on Tori.

Like the warm sunshine hitting my skin, I soaked in this perfect moment with my boyfriend and my best friends.

After a while, Emerson nudged me. "So, you wanna get outta here?" he asked quietly, a devilish grin on his face.

My smile reached my ears, and my stomach did several flips. "Okay," I whispered.

He took my hand and led me away. I glanced back at the ice cream shop, where my friends continued talking and laughing. Then I followed Emerson to the park down the street.

With only a week of summer left, there was so much I wanted us to do together, and I didn't want to waste a minute of it.

Under the shade of a tree, I watched him ride his skateboard. He fell a few times trying to land new tricks, but he got right back up and tried again. Unable to tear my eyes off of Emerson, I realized that life was just like that. Lots of falling and scraping of elbows and knees. Then getting back up anyway.

Emerson fell and got up again, brushing himself off. He was so much stronger and more resilient than he knew. Maybe he doubted it, but I would definitely remind him.

This summer, I'd tutored him through math and social studies, but in the end, Emerson had taught me to take risks with my heart.

After he finally nailed a new trick, he walked over to me. He held out his hand and helped me up.

"Come on," he said. "You should give it a try."

I shook my head. "You know I'm not very good at this."

"I always wanted a girlfriend who could keep up with me on a skateboard," he said, giving me a quick wink.

I laughed. "I'm not sure I'll ever be able to keep up with you on a skateboard."

"You won't know unless you try," he said with a smile.

It did look fun, even if there was a big risk I'd end up with a broken something.

Besides, it was an excuse to be close to Emerson.

So I put my foot on the skateboard and pushed off. I lost my balance, my arms flailing, sure I was going to fall. But then Emerson was there, his arms around me.

"I got you," he said. "I won't let you fall."

I stepped off the board and turned to face him. My eyes settled on his, and he put his arms around me, coming in close.

I let myself get lost in his sweet kisses, realizing that my summer had been pretty great after all.

———

WILL a game of truth or dare ruin their friendship—or turn it into something more?

Read Lena's story, #TheBoyfriendDare, now: https://www.amazon.com/gp/product/B07NSGCHW6/

AUTHOR'S NOTE

H ey :)
        You made it! <3

I can't believe I'm more than halfway done with this series. Time flies when you're having fun.

When I found out that Harper's story would be next, I'll confess that **I wasn't sure how I felt about writing her story.**

She's probably the character I relate to the least, honestly.

Not because of skin color but because of personality. Harper is simply 100% kind at heart, and I'm known to just say what's on my mind sometimes. Haha!

But her book has probably been the most fun for me to write up until now. Each book is, of course, in its own way, but this one just really got to me.

It ended up being so heartfelt and deep, and it was also incredible to write a good girl who falls for a bad boy! Talk about one of my favorite tropes.

Where did I get the inspiration for Harper and Emerson?

Harper and Emerson were in part inspired by **Jess and Rory from Gilmore Girls!**

While handsome Dean will always have a special place in my heart, **Rory and Jess's first kiss GETS ME EVERY TIME.**

It's seriously my favorite. **I knew I wanted to create something like that with Harper and Emerson.**

I also had a ton of fun researching skateboarding and parkour and finding out that skateboard parkour is a thing!

Next, I'll be diving into Lena's story, which… should be really interesting! ;)

If you want to know when that book is available, make sure you sign up for my newsletter and become a VIP reader :)

In the meantime, I'd love to hear what you thought of #GoodGirlBadBoy and which #BFF is your favorite.

Email me your thoughts and questions at hello@yeseniavargas.com. You can count on me to reply!

Book 4 Available Now!

Read Lena's story…

Will a game of truth or dare ruin their friendship—or turn it into something more?

Download #TheBoyfriendDare now!

Become a VIP Reader & Download Your Bonus Content!

Become a VIP Reader today and get access to all of your **exclusive bonus content**, including:

- the short story of how Baller929 and TheRealCinderella met (from Baller929's point of view!)
- exclusive sneak peeks of the next book in the series!
- Secret giveaways!
- plus fun updates & pictures of me and my kids you won't find anywhere else

My youngest daughter, Celeste, and me :)

You will be nearly as cool as Celeste once you sign up ;)

What are you waiting for? Become a VIP reader and download your bonus content today!

I'll send more pictures of my kids :) Promise.

Sign up right now at: www.yeseniavargas.-com/bff3

Don't Forget to Leave a Review!

If you enjoyed this book and would like to see more books from me, make sure to write a review **(just a couple sentences is okay)!**

Reviews help other readers find my books, so **thank you in advance!**

Once again, thank you for reading #Good-GirlBadBoy!

I'll see you in the next book :)

YESENIA

ACKNOWLEDGMENTS

Thank you once again to all of these amazing people:

My husband, who is a huge help and one of my biggest supporters.

My two amazing little girls, whose kisses and hugs sustained me these past several months. They more than made up for the constant interruptions :)

My best friend and biggest fan, Zendy <3 Your never-ending support and encouragement means the world to me.

My friend, fellow author, and editor, Kelsie Stelting, whose feedback and suggestions helped me level up this story (and continues to put up with my whining about not wanting to do edits).

My YA Chicks group of friends, including Sally, Cindy, and Kelsie. Thank you for all the feedback, support, and encouragement! And making Thursday nights fun :) Can't wait to hang out with you guys in person again!

My Thursday Night Inferno accountability group.

Your friendship, support, and encouragement means more than you know.

My cover designer, Jenny, who nailed this cover. Thank you so much for being a part of my team.

My VIP Readers and Awesome Review Team. Thank you so much for being patient, reading the story, and helping me spread the word about #GoodGirlBadBoy. You guys are my favorite :)

ABOUT THE AUTHOR

Yesenia Vargas is the author of several young adult romance books. Her love for writing stories was born from her love of reading and books. She has her third grade teacher to thank for that.

In addition to writing and reading, she spends her time hanging out with her family, working out, and binge-watching Netflix. In 2013, she graduated from the University of Georgia, the first in her family to go to college.

Yesenia lives in Georgia with her husband and two precious little girls. She also blogs at writermom.net

Check out what she's up to at yeseniavargas.com.

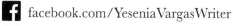

facebook.com/YeseniaVargasWriter

instagram.com/thisiswritermom

ALSO BY YESENIA VARGAS

#BestFriendsForever Series

#TheRealCinderella

#LoveToHateThatBoy

#GoodGirlBadBoy

#TheBoyfriendDare

#AllIWantForChristmas

Find all the download links as well as a complete list of my
most recent books at yeseniavargas.com/books/.

Made in the USA
Las Vegas, NV
20 November 2022

59905364R00120